THE

RED

BOY

T.M. Camp

Published in the United States of America
ISBN: 978-0-9825603-8-9

Cover & Interior Design by Kyle Harris
www.somethingpanda.com

--

Published by Aurohn Press
www.aurohnpress.com

For Steve and Ray, just because.

Dusk

The boy sat suspended in the air, listening to the creak of the chains, moving gently from side to side.

The wind was cold, the sky dark. He ought to be getting home.

He didn't want to leave. The playground was usually such a noisy place. During the day there was no quiet, no time to sit on the swings and just let the wind push him back and forth... back and forth.

By day, the playground was a rush of voices and bodies—the crowded thump of other children, voices stretched tight as a scream.

But not now... Now, he could hear the breath of the wind, the rustle of the leaves, the gentle click of the swings knocking against each other.

He out to be getting home. His mother would be worried.

But...

He just the couldn't bring himself to slip out of the swing, to slap his feet against the sand and break the spell of silence around him.

Not yet.

He wanted to wait, suspend the moment a while longer... make it last.

The boy leaned against the chain, cool across his cheek. The dark silhouette of the branches overhead framed the deeper dark of the sky beyond.

He did not see the red eye in the trees behind him—the cyclops glare of ember, the hot pulse of the cigarette.

The moment broke around him like glass—a frantic, jagged scramble… a thump of bodies… the thin stretch of his scream.

And then the playground was quiet once more—save for the sound of the empty swings, the branches overhead creaking in the wind.

SPRING

The children were screaming.

April could feel the baby shift inside her with every new outburst. She wondered what it might be thinking, what it could possibly understand of all this noise.

I'm going to have to get used to this sooner or later, she told the baby. *You might as well too.*

She adjusted, shifting her backside. The bench looked so comfortable when she sat down, worn smooth by previous generations of watchful mothers. She regretted not bringing along a pillow. She'd been avoiding the bathroom scale these past few months. She already felt like she had a built-in cushion. The bench proved her wrong.

She curled her lip. *Pregnant isn't fat,* she told herself.

The voice of her mother answered: *Ain't an excuse to let yourself go, either.*

The playground buzzed with life and noise. After being cooped up all winter long, everyone seemed desperate for the warmer weather. April saw the other mothers raising their faces to the sun, eyes closed, so grateful.

The children soaked it up as they ran, little dynamos. There was a madness in their play—clockwork toys set free after a good winding—bursts of chaos and activity, punctuated by their shouts and screams. April jumped every time a new cry rang out. Each one sounded to her like a horrible tragedy had just occurred, each one the end of the world.

But the other mothers barely looked up from their magazines or their gossip.

April twisted her mouth, wry. She was still trying to get used to that as well—being outside all the talk, feeling like it was directed at her.

A woman approached the bench and nodded. She had two puffy jackets tucked under her arm. "Is this seat taken?"

April shook her head. "Please."

The woman sat down, arranging the coats on the bench next to her. The slick nylon made them difficult to stack and, after two or three tries, she just let them slide to ground. She smiled at April and shrugged. "Can't get them to wear them anyway."

April nodded, though she didn't understand. Together the two of them watched the children run and climb. To April's eyes, they looked like a flock of starlings at twilight—moving to and fro without any logic or reason. But, she supposed, the trained eye of a mother could decipher and track those strange migrations.

"Do you mind?" The woman next to her held up a cigarette and a lighter.

April shook her head. "Not at all."

The woman sighed, wasting no time lighting the cigarette and taking a long, satisfied drag. She exhaled, squinting one eye against the smoke. "It's kind of like a visit to the zoo, isn't it?"

"Pardon?"

The woman gestured with her cigarette at the mass of children at play. "If we could just talk the city into putting bars around this place, we could all take the afternoon off."

April forced a smile. She understood that some women resented their children. But it still surprised her to see how much disregard—if not actual, outright dislike—many mothers seemed to have for their kids.

Something caught her eye, a fixed point in the swarm: A boy in a red sweater playing by himself in the sand, perfectly calm and at home in the chaos around him.

April couldn't help but like him for that, even envy him a little.

And then, without warning, she was coughing. The fit came over her so quickly, doubling her up. The woman sat up, concern flickering across her face. April wanted to assure her that she was fine, but all she could do was wave her hand feebly in the air between them.

The woman held her cigarette out at arm's length. "It's not..?"

Still coughing, April shook her head. "No, it's..." Another fit overtook her.

"I can put it out," the woman offered.

April noticed that she didn't actually do so. Still coughing, she managed to croak "No, no... I'm fine, honestly..." More coughing.

"You're sure?" The woman was already raising the cigarette for another drag. "Because it's..."

April managed to get herself somewhat under control. "No, thank you... just snuck up on me is all."

The woman settled back against the bench. "Are you going to be sick?"

April shook her head, not sure. "No, no... I'm fine. Really." She blinked a few times, clenching her jaw against the choke crouched at the back of her throat. "Thank you."

"Just let me know if you change your mind." The woman took a paperback out of her purse and began to read.

Gee, thanks... April gave the book a sidelong glance. The woman caught her peeking and April, a little embarrassed, smiled. "How is it?"

The woman made a seesaw gesture with her hand. "I liked the movie better. And I already know how it ends. So…"

Before April could reply, the woman rose and strode quickly to the edge of the playground where a little girl had taken a tumble at the bottom of the slide.

"Oh, sweetheart," the woman said, lifting the girl up. "Did you fall?"

The girl wailed, nodding. There was sand ground into both of her knees. Even from where April was sitting, she could tell it must be painful.

The little girl wrapped her arms around her mother, allowing herself to be carried back to the bench.

The woman set the girl down and knelt in front of her. "Let's take a look at the damage."

The little girl sniffled, shining snail tracks of tears smeared across her dusty cheeks. "Hurts…"

Her mother gently brushed the sand off of one knee. The girl flinched. "Ow…"

The woman pressed her lips together. "You need to hold still and let me…"

"…but it hurts," the girl protested. "I'm bleeding."

"So show me…" the woman began, but her daughter cut her off.

"I'm *bleeding*," she insisted.

The woman brushed at more of the sand—a little less gently this time, April noted. "Oh, I don't think so…"

"…it *hurts*." The girl drew the word out, almost to the point of absurdity.

April did her best not to smile.

The woman, however, was not impressed. "I'm sure it does, but it's just a little scrape and…"

"…I'm bleeding." The girl kicked at her mother's hands.

The woman sat back on her haunches. "So, if you're bleeding, maybe you shouldn't try to kick me when I'm helping you. Unless you want me to let you bleed to death?"

The girl slumped a little. "No."

"I beg your pardon?"

"No ma'am."

The woman regarded the girl for a moment. "So, are you sure? Because…"

"…I'm sure." The girl laid her hands out in desperation. "I need your help. Please."

"Yeah, you do. And don't you forget it, young lady." She leaned forward again. "So, let me take a look."

She took a tissue out of her purse and moistened it on her tongue, dabbing at the girl's knee. The child flinched at her touch and tried to turn away.

"That hurts," the girl wailed again.

"I know it does, sweetheart, but…"

"…ow…"

"…I'm almost done."

April could feel the brittle edge of the woman's patience, the little scrape at the end of that final word. She remembered it very well from her own mother, always on the cusp of losing it completely.

"I need a band-aid," the girl said.

"Do you?" Her mother dabbed again.

April recognized the danger in that voice. Even as a child she knew it, but was unable to stop herself from pushing her mother further.

As was the little girl, apparently. She nodded, sniffling for dramatic effect. "Uh huh."

The woman looked up at her daughter over the top of her sunglasses. "You need a band-aid?"

The girl nodded again.

"Oh, I don't think so."

"But I'm bleeding." The girl seemed genuinely shocked her mother couldn't see how obvious her peril was. "I need one."

Her mother stood up, stowing the tissue back in her purse. "So, when we get home, we can put one on it."

The girl kicked her feet. "I need one now."

"You do?"

"Yes."

It was clear to April that both mother and daughter were utterly disgusted with each other.

"So, we should go home then." The mother snapped her purse closed. "Right now."

She looked at the girl. "Right?"

The girl started to answer, then stopped.

"Because if you really need a band-aid," her mother went on. "Then we'll need to hurry home before you bleed to death."

Like a mask falling away, the girl's whole demeanor shifted. Calmly, respectfully, she asked "Can we come back? After?"

"Mm, probably not, sweetheart." Her tone was comforting, but her eyebrows arched. "So, do you still want to leave?"

"No."

"So you're sure?" Her mother asked. "Because I know how bad your knee must hurt and…"

"…it's fine," the girl said quickly, hopping down from the bench. "Can I go back and play some more?"

"*May* I go…'"

"…*may* I go back and play some more?"

"All right, then." The woman straightened up as her daughter ran off. She sat down, giving April a smile. Together they watched as the little girl displayed her wounds proudly for the other children.

The woman sighed, though with relief or exasperation April couldn't quite tell.

"She's very cute," April said.

"Thank you." The woman lit another cigarette. "So, when are you due?"

April took a breath, held it for a moment. *Now the questions.*

"Soon. End of June. But they keep saying not to make any plans, it could be sooner."

The woman nodded. "They always say that. They don't really know anything much at all. And with your first, all bets are off."

She knew, then. *How did she know?*

April was still on the outside, not quite a full-fledged, dues-paying member of the Mom Club yet. "Is it that obvious?"

The woman smiled, proud of her detective work. "A little."

"What gave me away?"

There was so much April had left to learn, all these little tricks that the other mothers seemed to know. Not for the first time, she wondered if there was a secret manual. She'd already decided long before that there must be a code that only mothers spoke—a secret society, all their little rituals.

And her, resentful and envious, outside.

The woman grinned, gestured with her cigarette to the clutter of coats and bags around her. "No stroller, no jackets to carry, no abandoned shoes and socks filled with sand."

The woman shook her head. "So, your hands are always going to be full—bunches of weeds that look like flowers but are really weeds. But that won't stop you from taking them home to put them in a glass of water on the kitchen windowsill just to let someone feel good for picking them for you."

The woman flicked her ash. "You'll find out soon enough."

She nodded to the children at play. "Start by learning to pretend to be patient. Noise and arguments and tiny little battles every second of the day. You'll surprise yourself with how much you can take… and with how horrible you can be when you hit your limit."

"Oh, I don't know…" April began.

"They will push every button you have. Even a few you didn't know were there. Just remember, when you go over the edge: They took you there."

Another flick of the ash, a fussy gesture that made April immediately anxious.

"So, you'll feel guilty. You'll be the worst mother in the world for an afternoon. Believe me, I know." She shook her head. "But kids need to learn what happens when you push someone past their breaking point. Otherwise, when they get out in the real world, they'll get destroyed. Boundaries are there for a reason."

April wanted very much to go somewhere quiet and cry for a few hours.

The woman chuckled, digging an elbow into April's side. "You'll find out soon enough."

April faked a smiled as best she could. "I expect I will."

"Count on it." The woman nodded. "So, how far along are you?" She shook her head. "Stupid question. You're due in June. I can do the math."

A scream from the playground. April looked up sharply but she could see nothing amiss. The children were only playing.

"False alarm." The woman hadn't even bothered to look. Apparently mothers could decipher the subtle differences between screams of delight and bloody murder. "So, at least you'll be done before summer really heats up. It's hell, being pregnant in August."

April figured it would be. Even with the chill of winter still lingering at the edges of the day, she felt overheated and faint most of the time. She couldn't imagine what those long, humid days would be like.

The woman stubbed out her cigarette. "So, how are you feeling?"

"Not too bad…" April could feel a knot of tears gathering in her throat, very tight. She wanted very, very much not to let it out. "The first few months were worse than I expected. But my doctor says I'm in the home stretch now, so…"

The woman scoffed. "Mm, they always say that. Doctors. They love making it sound easy, making you feel like you're just a hysterical woman. Worrying, making things worse than they are." She shook her head. "They act like they deliver a litter of puppies every damn day, like it's nothing, and scold us for saying we're tired or our tummy's upset."

"I suppose," April said slowly. "But, I mean, there's no use complaining."

The woman laughed. "I say complain all you want. It's the one time in your life when you've got a good reason, the one time when you deserve a little sympathy. Milk it."

She leaned in close to April, jerking her head toward the kids on the playground. "Believe me, take what you can while you can. Because once you have a few of these little monsters running around the house, no one will ever think to ask how you feel ever again."

She leaned back again. "Were you sick at all?"

"Oh… not really." April realized that she was close to one of the secrets, the key to that hidden code only mothers knew. Once you were one of them, you were in. "I did, I was, the first few months. Only once or twice, always right before breakfast…"

"…mm," the woman nodded. "I remember it well."

"And then, one morning at the beginning of my fourth month… nothing. It just went away."

The woman rummaged in her purse and pulled out a little plastic box of mints, offering one to April. "Mm, you're lucky. I was draped over the commode three times a day for seven months straight with Mary."

"Mary." April looked out at the playground. The girl hopped between a chain of rubber tires. *Mary.*

"What are you having?" The woman asked. "Boy or girl?"

April was beginning to like this woman. She was a professional. And if her questions were circling the boundaries of certain topics that April didn't want to cross—well, there was no stopping that.

"I don't know," she said.

"Couldn't they tell? Or didn't you want to ruin the surprise?"

April thought about the young woman, smearing the thick gel on her belly and running that unfortunate, embarrassingly shaped sensor back and forth—pressing in on her sides as though she were taking a physical imprint of the baby.

The nurse kept her eyes on the monitor in front of her, never once looked at April. "Will the father be joining us today?"

"They asked me if I wanted to know, but…" April shrugged. "I suppose that means they could tell."

"Mm, you'd be surprised." The woman daintily spat out the mint and tapped another cigarette from the pack. "A lot of it is just guesswork: 'This could be his penis or her pinky. No promises, no guarantees.'"

"Well…" April searched for the right response, the little joke that would confirm her place in the club.

She failed.

"So," the woman asked as she lit her cigarette. "Didn't you want to find out?"

No turning back now. "I didn't, no."

She braced herself for some kind of shock, some acknowledgement of this terrible transgression of protocol. Pregnant mothers were supposed to be obsessed with every little detail of their unborn child's life, weren't they? Any hint of ambivalence or, god forbid, outright reluctance— well, she might as well give up her membership card here and now.

"Stand up." The woman eyed her critically. "Let me look at you."

April got to her feet, wondering yet again if she would ever feel like the rest of society didn't own her, couldn't command her to answer their questions, stand up and show off her belly, let them lay their hand uninvited to sound the depths within.

The woman studied her for a moment, gestured for her to turn to one side.

"Mm, carrying high…" she said thoughtfully. "I'd say it's a girl."

April maneuvered herself back onto the bench. "I've always heard carrying high is a sign that it's a boy."

The woman shook her head. "No. Boys are low."

"Which were you?"

The woman tapped her ash—a clean, decisive gesture. "Mary was high. But my oldest was a bit of both."

Ah, April thought. *A veteran.* "Boy or girl?"

"Mm, boy…" The woman pointed to the swings. "There."

She called out to a boy who seemed to be a bundle of sticks and mischief, maybe eight years old. "Not too high, sweetheart."

If the boy gave any sign that he'd heard his mother, April didn't see it. He pumped harder with his legs, apparently trying to swing all the way over the top.

April smiled. "What's his name?"

"Gabriel." The woman arched an eyebrow. "Utterly ironic, I assure you. It seemed like a good idea at the time but, come to find out…"

She held out her hand palm up, like a magician revealing a wondrous trick. "We got this instead."

April thought he looked rather sweet, and said so.

"They always do," the woman replied. "When they're not yours."

As they watched, the boy vaulted from the very top of his arc, flying outward, out of the swing to sprawl face-first in the sand.

April gasped.

The woman didn't even bat an eye. "Utterly fearless." She took a long drag of her cigarette.

The boy hopped up and grinned through a crusted mask. He hawked out a remarkable amount of sand and spit. April saw that he glanced over to make sure his mother had seen before he ran back to the swings once more.

"Little monster," the woman muttered, the smoke trickling out with her breath. A proud dragon.

April smiled. She liked this woman, liked her sharp edges and matter-of-fact sense of humor. It was refreshing after all the playacting the other mothers seemed to do, trying to get cast in the role of the perfect mommy. "How old is he?"

"Ten. Going on thirty-five." The woman shook her head. "Do you and your husband have any names picked out?"

April did her best not to panic. "Not really. I think I'll wait and see who it is, see what name fits."

The woman considered the tip of her cigarette for a long moment. "So which do you think it is, boy or girl?"

"I honestly don't know. Sometimes I feel one way, but sometimes…"

"…which do you want?"

April came up short on the question. "Don't see how it matters, actually, what I want. It's going to be whatever it's going to be." She heard the bitter edge in her voice, tried to blunt it with a small laugh. Still sharp enough to hurt, though.

"No preference at all?"

April considered. "Sometimes… Sometimes I think a little girl would be sweet. Tea parties and Easter dresses and a doll house on Christmas morning."

"Mm," the woman nodded.

"But then I see a little boy in the grocery store, with his little shoes and serious face, all grumpy, slouching around like a little man and my heart kind of goes 'Oh…' You know?"

"I do."

"But I say, as long as it's healthy—he, she, whatever—long as they've got all their fingers and toes, it doesn't matter. I don't care. Just give me my baby, safe and sound."

April surprised herself, the force of her words. She swallowed against the knot, sudden in her throat once again.

"Absolutely right." The woman shifted in her seat to face April, thrust out her hand. "My name's Jan."

Jan. April shook the woman's hand. "April."

They turned back to watch the children once more.

After a long moment, Jan took a breath. Her voice was even, almost rehearsed. And as she spoke, her eyes never left her children.

"So, you're right, you know. Doesn't matter what they are, doesn't matter who they are—just so long as they're all right."

She paused a moment. "I lost my first, actually. Twelve years ago."

Another moment, a drag on her cigarette. "Before Gabriel. Gabriel's older brother."

April was suddenly very conscious that she had no idea where to look. She settled on a spot in the sand near them, a small pale twig poking up, scoured and bleached by time.

"Premature," Jan said evenly. "Bad heart. Didn't even get to hold him. Got one glimpse and then they just wooshed him off to the incubator. Never brought him back."

"How awful." April realized Jan already knew it was awful, she'd known how awful it was for twelve long years. And yet... this woman watched another son, a daughter grow inside her—always worrying, always wondering if they would make it through, if she would ever have the chance to hold them.

Awful was the least of it.

Jan shook her head. "I'm so sorry. I shouldn't be telling you all that. Last thing you need to hear..."

"...no, no. It's fine." April wanted to touch the woman, give her shoulder a squeeze, let her know that it was okay, let her know that she felt for her. But she just sat there, her fingers twisted together. "I'm not worried at all. It's fine, really."

Jan's face went sour, turned inward. "Mm, always hated that. Everyone telling you their horror stories and if they don't say 'Aren't you scared?' then they say 'Isn't it exciting?' And all you want to do is strangle them."

She reached for her cigarettes, thought better of it. "Drove me crazy with my first, all the attention and questions and advice…"

She stopped and looked at April. "So there I go again. I'm sorry."

"It's fine, really."

"Well." Jan wasn't ready to let herself off the hook.

"I have thought about that, though." April told her. "I guess it's normal to worry about something going wrong." She looked down at the swell of her strange, familiar body. She wondered if afterward she would miss it—this new planet, splitting off from her orbit.

"I guess there's no use worrying," she said. "It doesn't help anything."

Jan laid her hand on April's. "You shouldn't, shouldn't worry. I almost got scared off of the whole thing for good but, well, it all worked out in the end. Mary and Gabriel… Gabriel and Mary."

She said it as though she'd said it before, many times. A mantra late in the night, a child's prayer to keep shadows away.

"Mary and Gabriel." April desperately wanted to nudge the subject in a different direction. "Are those family names?"

"Mary, Gabriel, Stephen…" Jan shook her head. "Sixteen years of Catholic school makes an impression, let me tell you."

"Stephen?"

"Stephen was my first." Rehearsed, matter-of-fact.

April nodded, at a loss.

"Don't worry," Jan told her. Again.

"I don't," April waved off the concern as best she could. "Not really.

They say everything is fine but…"

But some nights I get into bed and realize that I can't remember the last time I felt a kick or… I just lie there and wait… hoping for a shift, some movement, anything to let me know everything's okay. It always comes… I'm half asleep and there's a kick. And then I'm wide awake—but grateful.

She didn't know how to say any of this.

Jan seemed to understand. "Get used to it."

"I feel like I'm being teased sometimes." April wanted to make a joke of her worrying, failed. "Like the baby's doing it on purpose."

"If it isn't yet," Jan laughed. "It will be soon enough. Wait until later, when the kid really masters the art of pushing your buttons. You've no idea."

"Oh, I'm sure I'll find out."

"You will, don't worry." Jan nodded out at the playground. "So the thing I dread right now is high school. In a few years, Demonspawn over there will start dating. I shudder to think about setting him loose on young, impressionable girls."

April watched as the boy tore through the playground, a force of nature. He wasn't yet able to even notice the girls around him but, she saw, a few noticed him. With his dark hair and bad-boy antics, he was well on his way to being a heartbreaker.

April knew the type. Too well.

"Just like his father," Jan muttered. She looked over to April, half-rose in her seat. "Oh my goodness, are you all right?"

April nodded, eyes closed. "Just a little…" she breathed heavily for a moment. Her hands were braced against the seat of the bench and she could feel the sudden sweat on her face. She shook her head, flushed, praying the moment would pass soon.

Jan waited.

April let out a long breath, held it for a moment. Then she let it out again, carefully. "I'm sorry."

"Are you all right? Braxton-Hicks?"

April shook her head again. "I don't know, really. I was folding some laundry this morning and my hips just…"

She didn't have the words to describe what had happened, the way her skeleton seemed to suddenly shift inside her, the bones of her pelvis clicking into a new shape. "I've just been achy, my hips… I feel like they're coming apart… which, I guess, they probably are."

Jan snorted. "If they didn't, we'd never survive."

April opened her eyes, the moment passing. "Did you ever feel that? Like your bones just opened up about three more inches?"

"I didn't, no." Jan shrugged. "But everybody's different. And being pregnant is strange. I know some women who love it. Idiots."

"Really?" April hadn't heard this before.

"A friend of mine says it's the best she's ever felt about herself and her body." Jan gave April a sidelong look. "Not me. Even leaving out the labor, I hated every moment of it. Fortunately, I'm all done."

"You are?"

Jan nodded. "You better believe it. Two's plenty. And those two…" she gestured out to the playground. "They're more than enough. Tom—that's my husband—he likes to say that all we need is one more and we'll have one of each: boy, girl, hermaphrodite."

April laughed in spite of herself. "That's terrible."

"He is terrible. Look what he's set loose on the world." Jan reached for her cigarettes. "What about your husband?"

The question hung in the air. April knew she waited just a moment too long before she replied. "My husband."

Jan tapped out a cigarette and fitted it between her lips. "So, he holding out for a boy or a girl?"

April shrugged. "I don't know what he wants. He didn't want a baby at all, so…"

She tried very hard not to think of him, the angry mix of shame and blame in his voice. "So he didn't want me either, once we found out."

She brushed her hair behind her ears, sweeping it back from her neck to catch a breeze. "No promises, no guarantees."

"I'm sorry," Jan said.

"Don't be." April made herself sound stronger than she felt. "It was months ago. So long as we have all our fingers and toes, everything will be fine."

"I should leave well enough alone. I'm just nosy like the rest of these bitches." Jan flung the last word at two women sitting nearby, didn't bother to lower her voice. "Trading drama and gossip, looking for clues."

"Clues?" April cocked her head. She was glad to hear someone else felt the same way about the other mothers, glad to know she wasn't the only one.

Jan patted the pile of coats next to her. "Clues. Shoes and jackets and flowers." She looked at April. "No wedding ring. No offense."

"None taken." April looked down at her hands. *Of course.*

She put them into the pockets of her coat. "You're not the first to notice, believe me."

"I bet. I'm sorry. I didn't mean to put you on the spot like that."

"You didn't." April told her. "Don't worry. I'll be all right."

"I'm sure you will."

They sat for a long while.

"I am a little..." April stopped, tried again. "I mean, I don't mind you asking. Most people don't, really. They don't ask... but they talk."

It was true. People watched her, she felt their eyes on her. She could see them talking, hear their voices drop when she walked past.

"And I don't like pain," she told Jan. "That's probably the only thing I'm scared of. I am not looking forward to that part of it at all."

"No one does," Jan told her. "But you'll be fine. It's a snap. Really."

"I know." April nodded, as much to herself as to the other woman.

"But it's still a bit scary. How long were you in..?"

Looking back, she was never entirely certain what happened—but it seemed like Jan had somehow disappeared. She was just… gone.

April had a split second of confusion before the scream from the playground. And then she saw Jan, already halfway to where her son stood howling.

The boy was incoherent, frantic to the point where April could hardly stand to watch as Jan tried to calm him down. The boy screamed and shook his hands in front of him, his face a mask of raw anguish.

In a clean, flat motion, his mother slapped him.

The boy's cries ceased immediately, if only momentarily. His eyes surged in his face and, even from where she was sitting, April could see his face boil bright red as a new wave of screams rolled over him.

His mother slapped him again.

Before he could explode once more, she took him by the arm and tore him free from the playground, marching him away from the rest of the children. His cries subsided, a repeating wave of hitches and sobs between which his mother tried to ask him questions.

She knelt down in front of him. "So what's wrong?"

"It… hurts," he gasped. "It hurts…"

"…what hurts?"

He gulped more air. "My hand…"

Jan took her son's hands in hers. "Which one? I don't see anyth…"

"…it hurts, it hurts, it hurts…" He was ramping up again.

"I don't see anything." Her voice, a crease in the air. "What happened?"

"…my hand…"

"…which one?" She grabbed his chin between her thumb and forefinger. "Sweetheart? Which hand?"

"This one…" He shook his left hand in front of her face.

She snatched it out of the air, looked it over. "I don't see…"

"…ithurtsithurtsithurts…"

April saw Jan tighten her jaw, the teeth clicked. "Did you smash it?" There was an impatience there. April thought of her own mother once more.

"No, it hurts…"

"…I know it hurts, sweetheart." That last word, like another slap. "Tell me what happ…"

"…it, no, this one… a bee, a bee stung it." He began to cry again.

"Show me where."

The boy shook his hand again. "Here… this one… it hurts…"

"…hold still." Jan held the hand up, inspecting it.

"He stung me."

She nodded. "He sure did. Come on."

She led him by the wrist back to the bench. April watched as she rummaged around in her purse. "All right, sweetheart…" Jan raised the boy's hand so he could see it. "So you see that right there? That's the stinger. See?"

The boy started crying again.

His mother plucked at his hand with her fingernails. "Look, I'm taking it out. You see? There. It's gone."

"It still hurts…"

April could see the woman was at the limit of her patience. "So, I know it does, sweetheart." She turned and rummaged in her purse.

"Do you need..?" April offered, having nothing that would help.

Jan waved her off. "No no, we're fine. Just another minor playground tragedy…"

She fished out her cigarettes and pulled a fresh one from the pack.

While April and the boy watched, Jan crushed up the cigarette in the palm of her hand. She took the tobacco and rubbed it into the boy's skin. He tried to pull away but she held him fast. "Listen, let me do this…"

"…it hurts. What is it?"

"So, it doesn't hurt and it's going to make you feel better. All right? It'll make it go away."

"What is it?"

Jan sighed, pressing the tobacco against the boy's hand with her palm. "One of mommy's cigarettes, sweetheart." She leaned back so he could see what she was doing. "Look, see how I'm holding it against the place where he stung you? Do you think you could do that for me?"

The boy nodded.

Jan took his other hand and placed it under her own. "So, hold it right there and press down tight, okay? Can you do that for me?"

The boy sniffled. "Yes."

Jan sat back on her haunches and looked at him for a moment. She rose and pulled him over to the bench.

"So, tell you what," she said. "Why don't you come and sit with me for a minute while you hold that on your hand. Okay?"

"Still hurts." But he allowed himself to be pulled over, tucked under his mother's arm.

"I know it does, sweetheart." She snuggled him in closer. "But let's just sit here for a minute and wait. All right?"

"All right."

They sat, watching the other children.

After a while, Jan asked "How you doing, tough guy?"

"All right."

"How's that hand doing? Feeling better?"

The boy nodded. April could see exhaustion in his face. All his wild energy punctured by the slender dart of a honeybee.

"You want to go play some more?"

He shook his head.

Jan squeezed his shoulder. She caught April's eye over the boy's head and gave her a wry smile. "It's not as hard as it looks."

"God, I hope not." April couldn't help but wonder if she would ever feel that in control. "I'm impressed."

"Don't be." Jan waved off the compliment. "Just an old trick. You pick them up as you go along." She covered the boy's ears with her hands. "Sometimes you just make something up, just to make them think you know what you're doing."

She let her hands fall again, tousled the boy's hair. She looked at April and shrugged. "No matter what you're ready for, there's always an accident on the way—some child-size tragedy you can't plan for or protect against. That's how it is. That's what it's like."

"Wonderful."

"Don't worry. You'll muddle through, same as the rest of us." She held up the boy's hand to inspect it. "So, let me see. Feel better?"

He nodded. "A little."

She sat back and looked at him with mock astonishment. "Just a little? It looks better than that to me. Do you want to go play some more?"

He considered for a moment. "No."

"You ready to go?"

"Uh huh."

She sighed. "All right, sweetheart. Let's collect your sister." Jan stood up and called in the general direction of the playground. "Mary! Time to go..."

April watched, fascinated. It was clear from her body language that the girl was doing her best to pretend she hadn't heard her mother's call.

Jan shifted slightly. "*Mary.*"

There was a weight to her voice, a resonance that carried over the sounds of the playground, impossible to ignore.

The little girl looked up. "*Mom...*"

The voice again. "Now."

Mary stomped over to the bench.

"I *am* impressed," April said.

Jan laughed. "It's all in the voice."

She picked up the jackets and held them out to her children. "All right, sweethearts: jackets."

While Mary and Gabriel struggled into their jackets, Jan said "Good talking with you. Sorry about all the horror stories."

"Oh, don't be," April said. "I've heard worse."

Jan zipped up the girl's coat. She touched April's shoulder. "So, you'll be fine. Good luck to you."

"It…" The knot again. "It was nice talking with you."

Jan inspected her children. "So, see you around, I hope. We come here quite a bit, don't we sweethearts?"

The children nodded.

Jan smiled. "It's a good place to play."

April nodded.

"Just watch out for the bees. And these bitches." Jan nodded at the other mothers. "See you soon."

She gathered her children to her. "So, come on then, sweethearts. Say good-bye."

The children mumbled, suddenly shy.

"Bye…" April raised one hand to them as they walked off.

After the crisis of the past few minutes, the noise of the children playing was comparatively quiet—peaceful, even. A relief.

April sat for a long while, trying to imagine what it would be like to come here with her own child, to sit and chat with Jan through days and weeks, watching as their children outgrew the mild dangers of this little world.

If the worst thing you have to worry about is bees… She'd been noticing more and more that she was speaking to the baby silently, as well as out loud. Just a few days earlier, she'd been in the grocery store stocking up on essentials and describing to the baby what each thing was and what it was for: "And these… these are wipes. That's how mommy will keep your bottom pink and clean."

It wasn't until later that she realized she'd been speaking aloud. The other shoppers probably thought she was more than a little bit of a loon.

I don't care, she told the baby. *Just so long as I have you.*

April shivered. The clouds had scoured the sun from the sky and the crowd of mothers and children was starting to thin out. Everyone was heading home for lunch.

She could feel the tension around her, overheard one woman say to another: "Hope the little brat takes a nap so I can have a few minutes for myself."

A nap sounded very nice right about now. The baby inside her lay dreaming. April longed to join them. She wanted nothing more in this moment than to curl up, enveloped in the gentle amniotic current and wrap herself around that warm little life, eavesdropping on softer dreams.

Lost in her thoughts, it was some time before April noticed that the playground was empty.

No, not quite.

There was one little boy still playing—it was the same boy she'd seen earlier, the quiet one in the red sweater. He looked young, perhaps seven or eight years old. She wasn't quite sure.

The boy was digging in the sand. He knelt, using his hands to scoop out a hole about a foot or so deep. After a while he moved on to a fresh spot. A new hole. And then on to another.

The playground was dotted with small pits here and there. It was obvious he knew what he was doing, so serious and determined.

He looked up at April, caught her staring. His eyes shot back down to the sand. After a few more handfuls, he moved on to a new spot.

He looked up at her again, began digging once more.

April stood up and went over to where the boy sat. She maneuvered her pregnant bulk down carefully, squatting next to him in the sand.

"Hello," she said.

The boy nodded, still digging. "Hello."

"Do you need any help?" April asked. "Did you lose something?"

The boy shook his head. "No ma'am."

April watched for a moment. "What are you digging for? Pirate treasure?" She was a little disappointed when he didn't seem nearly as excited as she pretended to be.

He sat back on his haunches and shook his head. "Bones."

"Really?" She tried to play it off as a joke. "Eeew…"

The boy looked at her. She felt a little jolt of something. His eyes met hers. She'd never seen a little kid so serious. She shifted slightly and stood up, pretending to stretch.

Truth was, though, she had an urge to back up and walk away from the boy. Never look back. Never come back again.

There was something slightly off about him, disconcerting.

Unnatural.

"Do you want to help me?" he asked her.

"Sure…" she said, drawing the word out, wishing she'd thought of some kind of excuse. But it was too late and, oddly enough, when she saw the boy smile, it made her feel a little ashamed of herself. He was just a little boy, after all.

"So, um… where should I start?" She looked around for an open spot.

The boy in the red sweater pointed to a bare patch in the sand a few feet away. "Over there, maybe?"

April went over and carefully sat down, crossing her legs as best she could. "Here?"

The boy nodded. "That'll work."

She watched as he returned to his digging. After a moment, she scooped a small hole in the sand. "Am I doing it right?"

The boy eyed her critically. "You've got to push the sand out of the way more, like this." He demonstrated. "Otherwise, it'll all fall back in again."

What an odd little kid. "How's this? Better?"

"Yes ma'am." The boy tilted his head to one side. "Sort of."

It was clear he didn't want to hurt her feelings.

"You're very polite," April told him. "What's your..?"

"...are you going to get a baby?"

April smiled. "Uh huh. I am."

"When?"

"Oh..." April had no idea when kids learned about this sort of thing. "Soon."

But the boy wasn't going to let her off the hook so easily. "When?"

"Summertime."

"When?"

Later, April would not be able to explain—even to herself—why she didn't want to tell this little boy about her baby. It puzzled her, this easy evasion.

She took a breath. "Sometime in June, maybe."

"What day?"

April held her ground. "Actually, I don't know the day. No one does. We won't know until it happens."

The boy considered this for a moment. "Thirty days hath September, April, June, and November."

April nodded. "That's right."

"I can count to thirty," the boy told her.

April put on her impressed face. "Can you?"

He nodded. "I can do it backwards. Do you want to hear me?"

Before she could answer, he was digging again—counting down the numbers with each new handful of sand.

April noticed that he transposed a few numbers as he counted. She didn't correct him.

When he was finished, April applauded. "Very good."

"I can do more," the boy told her. "It's easy. You just take away one and then another one, until you get to the end." Clearly, this was a deep secret of the universe—at least, of *his* universe.

Before she could think of a suitably awed response, the boy went back to digging.

Watching him pulling out handfuls of sand, she realized that it was a chore for him. He wasn't playing. He wasn't having fun.

"Two."

April cocked her head to one side. "Pardon?"

Still digging, the boy said "His birthday's on two. I think. The day."

"Who's birthday?"

"Your baby." He said it so matter-of-factly, it took a few moments for it to sink in.

"Oh, really?" April put her hands on her hips. "You sure it's a boy, are you?"

He looked at her like she was an idiot. "He is a boy."

"Well," she slipped back into that odd feeling again, an inexplicable compulsion to protect her baby. "Maybe he is, maybe he isn't."

"He is."

The boy when back to digging.

April scraped a few handfuls of sand out of her neglected little hole. "You know, even the doctors don't know for sure. They have to guess."

"Really?" The boy looked up at her. "Why don't they know?"

April had to admit it was a good question. "I don't know, actually."

The boy thought for a moment. "When you have him, after he's born, will you bring him back to play with me?"

April smiled, in spite of her misgivings. "Well, he will be just a little baby—at least, at first."

The boy nodded. Obviously. "But when he's bigger? Will you bring him? Can he come and help me dig?"

"But what if he's not a boy? What if he turns out to be a little girl?"

The boy's eyes searched her face, as though she'd said something very, very puzzling.

After a long moment, April relented. "Well… you might be right. Tell you what, will you promise me something?"

"Yes ma'am?"

"If you're right and it turns out to be a boy…"

"…he is a boy…"

"…well, if he is, I promise to bring him back to play when he's big enough. But you have to promise me to go home soon."

The boy nodded and resumed his digging. "But not when he's a baby, because babies can't dig."

April shook her head in agreement. "Nope. Not much they can't."

"Nope."

The boy said something else, but April couldn't make it out.

"What was that?" she asked him. "What did you say?"

"Then we can dig. Me and Jimmy."

April was at a loss. "Jimmy?"

"Pardon?"

She knew the answer, knew what he would tell her now… but she couldn't help herself. She had to ask. "Who's Jimmy?"

He nodded to the globe she'd been carrying around her midsection for the past seven months. "The baby."

"You think his name is Jimmy?"

"Yes ma'am." He could hear it in her voice, she could tell. Somehow he knew she was on her guard.

"Who says?"

The boy shrugged. "It just is, I guess."

Are all little kids this creepy?

Suddenly, the playground had gone cold.

Without trying to make a big deal out of it, April stood up and stretched again.

The boy looked up at her. "Are you leaving now?"

She nodded. "I have to go. Are you ready?"

The boy shook his head. "No ma'am."

"No?"

"Not yet."

April didn't know if this was her maternal instinct kicking in, but this odd child, there was something in his manner that resonated deep within her. She could feel a tug there, a pull. Responsibility.

And there was fear there as well—though it was much later before she found herself wondering if she was afraid for him... or of him.

"Shouldn't you go home?"

"Not yet," the boy said again.

"Well..." April cast about for a moment, trying to channel the same kind of logic that Jan had used with her children. "Well, all the other kids are gone."

The boy stopped and looked up, surveying the empty playground.

He resumed digging.

"Well, I should be going." April didn't expect much of a response, and didn't get one. "Won't you be scared, all alone?"

"No ma'am."

April decided to try one last time. "Look, I don't think it's a good idea for you to be here all by yourself."

"Why not?"

"It's not safe."

The boy shrugged. "I'm here all the time by myself."

April sighed. "All right, then."

This was not her child. She couldn't force him to leave if he didn't want to go. She stood a moment longer, but the boy continued to dig.

So she went to the edge of the playground, stopping just outside the concrete ring that bordered it on all sides. She looked back.

The boy was watching her.

"All right, then," she said again.

The boy got up, dusting off his hands on his sweater. The damp sand clung to the thick wool of his sleeves, very pale against the red.

He stood just inside the concrete border. "Good-bye."

"'Bye," April said. "Thanks for letting me dig with you."

He nodded. "Thank you for helping me."

"I'm sorry we didn't find any bones."

The boy shrugged. "I'll keep looking."

April shivered. The sky was layered with clouds. She could feel the promise of rain, the damp and the chill in the breeze.

Winter isn't done with us yet. "Are you sure you're not supposed to be getting home?"

"No ma'am." He was the politest child April had ever met. "I can't leave, not yet. Not until I find all my bones."

"Won't your mother, won't your mom be worried?"

The boy said "She knows where I am."

"You should go home, though. Eat some lunch."

He shook his head. "I can't leave." He said it like it was a rule, like he'd get into trouble if he disobeyed.

"Okay, then," April said. "But now, listen: Promise me you'll go home once you find some bones? You can show them to your mom... I bet your mother, I bet she would like to see them."

The boy seemed unconvinced. "Maybe."

"Promise, though?"

He nodded.

She narrowed her eyes. "Well... alright, then. I'll see you later."

The boy perked up. "When you bring Jimmy? When he's bigger?"

"I suppose."

"Promise." The boy's eyes on hers, very green.

"I promise." She turned to go. "You be careful."

"Yes ma'am."

"See you."

The boy waved. "Good-bye."

April walked along the concrete path that led out of the playground. At the end, where it joined the sidewalk and the street beyond, she looked back.

The boy was digging again.

Even at a distance, she could hear that he was counting.

This was, she realized later, the first time she felt like a mother.

She smiled and turned away, heading for home.

SUMMER

Jimmy waited in the darkness, his breath echoing around him. The air inside the tunnel was warm, heavy. He didn't dare leave.

If he finds me, I'm dead.

He held his breath, swallowing, the sound of blood in his ears. The curved walls around him—every sound, every movement he made resonated up and down the length of the tube, betraying him.

Outside, he could hear them counting.

He was almost out of time. "Quit peeking!"

"I'm not!" That was Adam.

"Cheater!" Another voice. Michael hiding somewhere else in the playground.

Adam again, louder now. "I'm not cheating."

Jimmy knew that the more they called out, the easier it would be for Adam to find them. Their best chance was to delay the countdown, fluster the other boy.

The counting began again. But it was Michael who beat him to the next gambit: "Start over!"

The counting stopped. "What?"

Jimmy edged his way to the end of the tube. If Michael could draw all the attention, piss off Adam enough to hunt him down first, then Jimmy'd have no problem finding a new place to hide—one that neither of the other boys knew about. Now might be the time to give it a shot.

Michael and Adam were still in a shouting match, accusations flying back and forth. Jimmy grinned in the dark.

Michael won out. Jimmy heard Adam restart his count.

Time to make his move. He slid out of the tube, skinning his knee on the rough edge of the concrete lip. He called out, "Hey, slow down!"

He could see Adam on the other side of the playground, his arms over his face, leaning against one of the posts on the jungle gym.

Over to his left, Michael shouted "Count slower!"

"I am!" Adam dropped his arms.

Jimmy ducked behind the tube, hoping he hadn't been seen. "No peeking!"

"Cover your eyes!" Michael again, sounding close. Jimmy figured he was hiding in the little playhouse on the side of the playground. Again. Michael didn't have a lot of imagination.

"Start over!" Jimmy duck-walked around the far side of the tube. He resisted the urge to peek over the top to see if Adam was watching.

"And don't count so fast, cheater!" Michael shouted.

"I'm not! Jeez…" A long, annoyed moment passed. Adam began counting again.

Jimmy made a break for it.

He straightened up and ran as fast as he could to the far side of the playground. Out of the corner of his eye, he saw that Michael was switching hiding places as well.

Adam was counting down, halfway to zero now.

Jimmy slid to a stop near the old rusted swings, where years of sneakers had dug long, deep ruts in the ground. He lay down in one of these and began pulling loose sand and woodchips in over top of his legs and torso, burying himself.

Adam hit the final ten and finished his countdown by shouting, "Apple, peaches. pumpkin pie! Whoever's not ready, holler 'Aye!'"

Silence.

"Ready or not, here I come!"

Jimmy pulled more sand over himself. He realized that he'd misjudged the depth of the rut, that he wasn't going to be able to bury himself completely.

There was an old newspaper fluttering against one of the supports of the swingset. He stretched out as far as he could and just managed to snag it between two fingers.

Over on the other side of the playground, he heard Adam shout, "Here!"

Michael was captured. "Jesus," he complained. "I thought that was a good spot."

It was, Jimmy thought to himself. *The first fifty times you hid there, dumbass.*

He could hear them, on the hunt now. Jimmy wondered if Michael had seen him switch hiding places.

He spread the newspaper over his head and chest, holding it in place with one hand tucked up against his armpit. With the other hand he did his best to finish covering himself.

He froze. He could hear them, close now. He tried not to breathe too hard. He could feel sand trickling in around his ribs and down the back of his jeans.

Footsteps nearby. Close.

He held his breath, expecting at any moment to feel someone grab him, waiting for the shout and discovery.

After a long moment, they moved off once more.

Jimmy waited. They might be trying to trick him. He heard them talking, off to his left. There was a shout and he heard Michael yell, "Gotcha, fucker!"

His curiosity got the best of him and he lifted the edge of the newspaper to peek.

Adam and Michael were over by the concrete tubes where he'd been hiding before. There was another boy with them, a little kid in a red sweater. The older boys thought they'd caught Jimmy.

He heard them apologize. The little kid ducked back into one of the tubes. Jimmy let the edge of the paper fall once more.

After a minute or so, Michael called out: "Olly, olly oxen free!"

Adam chimed in. "Come out, come out, wherever you are!"

"Hey, asshole," Michael shouted. "Game over!"

Closer now. Adam called "You win!"

Jimmy waited for them to come to him.

"Jimmy!" They sounded like they were maybe ten feet away. By the sound of their voices, they were facing away from him with their backs to the swings.

"Hey!"

"You think he left?" Adam asked.

Michael snorted. "Nah, he's just being a dick."

"Jimmy! Stop being a dick and come out!"

"Yeah! Game's over!"

They waited.

"Screw this," Michael said. "Let's go."

And that was when Jimmy rose up out of the sand, just as the two boys turned to leave. He let out a hollow moan, contorting his face as the newspaper and sand fell away. "Bwaaaaarrcgghhgghh!"

"Holy fuck!" Michael was in front of him, had just turned to face him. One more step and he would've been walking right on top of Jimmy.

"Jesus!" Adam jumped back, his hands cupped to his crotch like someone had grabbed his nuts and given them a good, strong twist.

Jimmy cracked up, laughing so hard that he could barely breathe.

Michael shoved him.

Jimmy went over backward, stumbling into the trench. His head bounced hard against the packed soil. The summer afternoon shot through with streaks of black and purple.

"You asshole," Michael kicked sand in Jimmy's face.

"Hey," Adam said, always the peacemaker. "Knock it off, guys."

Jimmy was up on his feet, spitting sand and spitting mad. He could feel the heat of the day against the top of his head, the sore spot throbbing where he'd struck it.

All he could see was Michael's face. All he could hear was the rush of blood in his ears.

But Michael was bigger than Jimmy. Six months older, too. He had an extra head of height and twenty pounds on him at least.

Jimmy had the heat of his own anger, but that could only get you into a fight. Once you were in it, you were on your own.

Soon enough, it was over.

Michael had Jimmy pinned, sitting on his chest with his knees on the boy's arms.

Utterly defenseless, Jimmy writhed, spitting like a bag of cats. And just as helpless.

Michael help up his hand. "You finished?"

Jimmy raged.

Michael slowly folded his hand into a fist. He cocked his head, said more firmly this time: "You finished?"

Jimmy howled and bucked. "Get off of me you fucking asshole."

"Not until you calm the fuck down." Michael's arm was tense, at the ready.

Adam stood to one side, utterly worthless. "C'mon, you guys..." but it was far too late for that sort of thing.

Jimmy screamed up at Michael again.

"I said shut up," Michael told him. "If you don't calm down…"

Jimmy threw himself back and forth, completely lost now.

"Jimmy?" Michael waited a moment. "Jimmy? If you don't calm down…"

"…fuck you…"

"…you don't knock it off, I'm going to…"

Jimmy let loose another torrent of rage and cursing.

Michael looked at Adam and, with a shrug, said, "I warned him…"

Pain bloomed between Jimmy's eyes, eclipsing everything—a red cloud passed over the world, thick and harsh. He rolled on the ground, gasping and clutching his bloodied nose.

Michael stood and brushed off his jeans, shaking his head. "Fucking asshole."

"You fucking…" Jimmy tried to get up, but one knee buckled. "You fucking hit me."

"No shit, Sherlock." Michael put his hand on Adam's arm, holding him back. "Don't bother, the little shit'll just…"

"…fuck you." Jimmy looked up from his cupped hands, filling with blood. "Look at this shit…"

Adam shook off Michael's hand and bent down, reaching for Jimmy.

"Fuck you." Jimmy pushed the boy away, smearing blood across Adam's T-shirt.

"Jesus…" Adam stepped back. "What's your fucking problem? I'm just trying to help."

"Don't need your fucking help." Jimmy got up slowly, pushed Adam away again.

"What're you pushing me for? I didn't…"

"…don't fucking touch me."

Adam doubled Jimmy up around his fist, putting him down again. Everyone was surprised by this, Adam most of all.

"Shit," Michael said, half laughing. "Jesus, cool it."

"Fuck you, Jimmy." Adam pointed down at the boy, full of righteous pissed-off-ness. "Fuck. You."

"Come on," Michael said, pulling at Adam's arm. "Fuck this faggot."

Adam stood there a moment longer, then turned. "Yeah. Fuck him."

Jimmy watched them walk away, too weak to call after them. The rage was trickling out his mouth in shallow breaths, all sand and spit.

He lay there, listening to the heat buzzing around him. He could see little specks glint in the sand. Despite himself, he wondered what they were.

He heard a crunching sound, footsteps approaching across the sand. "Fuck you."

He closed his eyes. When he opened them again, he saw a boy in a red sweater standing a few steps away. The boy was maybe three or four years younger than Jimmy. He looked a little scared.

Jimmy felt his throat clench, crusted with sand and dust and blood. He began to cough and it was a very, very long time before he stopped. He hawked a mass of grit and phlegm into the sand and looked up at the boy.

"What?" Jimmy didn't really need anyone staring at him. "Fuck you want, kid?"

The boy's mouth worked for a second, chewing his lip. "Are you all right?"

Jimmy grinned, teeth grinding on sand. "I am fucking fantastic."

He rolled over and pulled himself into a sitting position. His stomach was burning outward from the center, like the map on Bonanza.

"You're bleeding."

"No shit, Sherlock." Jimmy pulled his T-shirt up over his head and dabbed at his face. "My mom's gonna fucking kill me." It was a new shirt. It was now also pretty well fucked up. He shook his head, wiped his face as best he could. He looked up at the boy. "I get it all?"

The boy shook his head.

"Shit." Jimmy scrubbed his face, trying to think of some kind of excuse he could use to deflect the shitstorm that was guaranteed to rain down on him when he got home. It wouldn't be the first time he came home shredded. "How about now?"

The boy shook his head again.

Jimmy sat a moment, staring at the bloody shirt bunched in his hand. "Jesus. I give up."

He looked up at the little boy again. "What're you doing?"

The boy shrugged. "Digging."

"For what?"

The boy put his hand into his pocket and held something out to Jimmy.

At first, Jimmy thought it was an old stick. But then he realized it was a bone. He turned it over in his hands, ran his finger along the familiar curve. "Cool."

"It's a rib." The boy in the red sweater touched the left side of his torso. "From here. Do you want to help me dig?"

"I know what it is," Jimmy said. He handed it back to the boy and stood up, shaking out his shirt before he pulled it back on over his head. "Where should I start?"

The boy looked up at him, considered, and pointed past the swings where the trees crowded in at the edge of the playground. "Over there."

Jimmy nodded. "Gotcha." He went over and knelt down, throwing handfuls of sand back between his legs with both hands.

The boy in the red sweater watched him for a long moment. He went to the edge of the little trench Jimmy had dug earlier and knelt down, careful as he pulled the loose sand and dirt away.

They dug for a while. But pretty soon the heat caught up with Jimmy. He could feel the blood caked on his upper lip and around his nostrils. He glanced over once or twice at the other kid. It felt nice to have someone there with him, someone who wouldn't give him shit.

He wished he had a younger brother, sometimes.

"Hey?"

The boy stopped and looked up.

Jimmy held out his hand. "Can I see it again?"

The little boy got up and came over.

"Aren't you hot in that thing?" Jimmy couldn't believe the kid was wearing a sweater in the middle of the summer.

"No." The boy shook his head.

"Man," Jimmy panted. "I'm sweating like a monkey."

The little boy held out the bone and Jimmy took it from him, turning it over in his hands. "Where'd you find this? Over here?"

The boy pointed. "Under the swings."

Jimmy nodded, impressed. "Got any more?"

The boy dug into his pockets, handing over a few more. "This one's a finger, or part of a finger. It got broken."

He handed over another one. "This is another rib, from lower down."

He dug into his pocket again, held out a little nub of something in his palm. "This is a tooth, one of my back ones. I think"

"Pretty cool." It was a tooth, all right. A baby tooth. Jimmy could see the prongs of bone sticking out of the bottom, like a little crown. "You think there's any more?"

The boy in the red sweater nodded.

Jimmy handed the bones back. "Pretty cool."

He started digging again, his troubles at home forgotten. All he thought was how cool it would be to find a bone, take it home and put it on the bookshelf in his room where he kept special little things. Artifacts.

"You know," he said to the boy. "Did you know that babies are born with like two hundred and sixteen bones but when we grow up, we only have two hundred and six?"

The boy shook his head. "Where do the bones go?"

"Some of 'em grow together when you get older." He sat back and tapped his head. "Like, your skull starts off with four or five different bones and then after a while they kind of melt together into one big thing and that's your skull."

The boy said nothing. Jimmy went back to digging.

"Women have one more rib than men do. Because of Adam and Eve, you know?"

The boy shook his head.

"Because when God made Adam, he put him to sleep and took a rib out to make the woman, Eve," he explained. "So that's why they have more ribs than we do. They're made of bones, I guess."

This little scrap of wisdom lodged in between the teeth of his mind after his mom had gone through a church phase a few years ago. One of those things that he poked at with his mind from time to time. Eventually it would loosen and fall out... or fester and a little shred remain, rotting the edge of his memory.

He sifted the sand in his fingers, checking a few pebbles. "But we're made out of dust. Which I guess means bones are too, in the end. And that's why when you die and they bury you, your body turns to dust."

"Except for the bones."

"No..." Jimmy shook his head. "I'm pretty sure your bones turn to dust too, if you wait long enough."

"Two hundred is a lot," the boy said.

"Yeah." Jimmy saw tears in the boy's eyes. "You okay?"

"I only have these." The little boy looked down at the bones cupped in his hands. "I don't think I can find the rest of them before they turn to dust."

"How long have you been looking?"

"I've been digging a long time."

"Let me see those again?" Jimmy held out his hand.

The other boy stood there, unmoving.

"You think there's any more here?"

The boy nodded. "I know there are."

Jimmy shivered. This kid was starting to give him the creeps.

"Well," he stood up. "Thanks for letting me help out."

He dusted off his jeans. "Maybe you'll find more, whatever they are."

"They're bones. I told you."

"Right." Jimmy inspected his shirt, picking at the dried blood and sand. "Well, wherever they came from... I don't know. Maybe they're worth something. You could sell 'em to a museum or something."

This had occurred to him while he'd been digging. Money was one of those things you either had or didn't. And he didn't, so it was something he thought about the way a drowning man thinks about oxygen: Always, until he dies.

"So... see you later, maybe." He turned but the boy's voice stopped him.

"They came from a boy," the kid told him. "He was playing and somebody... somebody caught him here." The boy swallowed, pointed over to the swings. "There was no one around and... and then all of a sudden there was a man in the trees."

Jimmy turned to look, as though the man might still be there.

"The man pulled the boy down and hit him and hurt him and, and, and, and... and burned his skin with cigarettes and, and, and then he choked him and pushed a knife into his heart. It was very cold."

Jimmy turned back to the kid. "You making this up?"

"He took the body back into the trees and he, he cut it up and..."

The boy pressed his fingertips into his eye sockets, like he had a piece of grit there. His jaw worked. Jimmy could hear the boy's teeth grinding.

"And, and, and buried the bones all over so no one would find out what he'd done to the boy. So no one would catch him."

"What happened to the man?"

"I don't know."

This fucking kid, Jimmy thought to himself, *is all kinds of crazy.*

He didn't believe a word of it. It sounded like something kids tell to scare each other on the playground. Maybe one of them found a bone one day, made the whole thing up and it just spread. Maybe it was something a mom made up, to keep kids from staying out too late.

"Lemme see those again." Jimmy reached over and took one of the bones from the little boy's outstretched hand. He held it up to the light, inspecting it. "What's this one again?"

"It's the middle bone, from here..." The boy held his hand up, pointing to the space between the first and second knuckle on his index finger. "Right here."

Jimmy shook his head. "It's too short."

"It broke," the boy told him. "It broke when he pulled me off the swing and my hand got stuck in the chain and, and it got all twisted up and the man pulled and my finger broke, it broke..."

Jimmy stared at the boy.

The boy put his hand over his mouth. His fingers curled around his cheek—one finger oddly bent.

Jimmy wanted to throw himself out of the way, dive out of the path of whatever was rushing towards him. But he was frozen, transfixed. And all he could do was stand there and watch it come, listening to the boy.

"I heard it break before I felt it and I, I didn't... I started to cry and he put his hand over my mouth. His hand was sweaty and his fingers smelled like cigarettes and his mouth was hot against my ear and he was talking so fast, I didn't understand anything and, and, and then something hurt me, it hurt so bad and he wouldn't stop and I could smell the pine trees, like Christmas... And then I couldn't leave..."

"...Jesus, shut the fuck up." Jimmy thrust the bone back into the boy's hand with the others, knocking them all to the ground.

The boy picked them up, putting them back into the pockets of his pants. The last one, he held for a moment. "This," he said, "this was my rib. This one, from right here." He touched his side. "Right under my heart. See?"

He held up the curve of bone for Jimmy to see. "See right there? That's from the knife. He tried to pull it back out but it was stuck and he said a bad word like the one you just said and he twisted it and it scraped the bone, right here, and then there was so much blood and I died and then…"

"…shut the fuck up, please." Jimmy was backing away now, the muscles in his face twitching out of control.

"And I couldn't go home," the boy continued. "I couldn't leave, not without…"

"…shutupshutupshutup…"

"…not before I find my bones again…"

Jimmy spun away and fell to his knees, panting.

He vomited over himself, the sour stink rising in the heat. His jeans clotted with it. His mind, wild now: *Guess I don't need to worry about my bloody shirt anymore.*

"I'm sorry, Jimmy."

He heard the boy behind him, could feel him there. A shadow in the sun, radiant with cold.

Jimmy wondered how the little boy knew his name.

That got him up on his feet, running as fast and far as he could. And it was a long time before he stopped.

He ran until he couldn't hear the boy anymore… calling after him, calling his name.

AUTUMN

Kelly was pissed off.

Ever since she was a little girl, she always had high hopes for Halloween. There'd been a family on her street that put on a haunted house every year, taking groups of kids through their garage and backyard to look at homemade props and sets. They pulled out all the stops.

One year they did Frankenstein. There was a laboratory full of sparking equipment and bubbling tubes and, in the last scene, the monster rose up off the table and strangled the mad scientist.

That'd been a good year.

And then, the year she turned twelve, they did Dracula's castle. There was a spooky graveyard diorama and one of the fathers from the neighborhood—she never knew who it was—lurked in the shadows in a black tuxedo with a satin cape and fake teeth.

Kelly'd gone as a cheerleader that year, using her older sister's uniform and pom-poms. She'd had to stuff the bust with wads of toilet paper to get it to fit, of course. But fortunately it wasn't too cold that year, otherwise she would have frozen her ass off in the pleated skirt.

Cold as she was, Kelly was tingling all over. Halloween did that for her, ever since she was little. She would not have been able to tell you why.

But that night, that Halloween long past... she'd been aware of it, more than ever before. Maybe it was the rubber masks, moving like living faces as kids ran past. Or maybe it was the pleats of her starched skirt rubbing her thighs raw as the night wore on.

So when Dracula came up behind her in the dark, when he wrapped his cloak around her, when she could feel his teeth on the back of her neck and his hands crawling under her shirt... Well, All Hallow's Eve became her favorite holiday right then and there.

Twelve years old.

Standing out on the sidewalk afterward, her knees wouldn't stop shaking. She could still feel hot breath at the nape of her neck, the quick taptaptap of his fingertips playing across her ribs.

His fucking teeth. On her neck.

One moment in the shadows. Then he was gone. The monster.

She went back through three times that night.

After that, she had pretty high expectations for the holiday.

The following year, she stole her first kiss while she was trick-or-treating. She didn't even know the kid. She just grabbed him as he was walking past and dove into his face.

She left a green smear of lipstick across his mouth, like poison. Like a curse.

He was Batman. She was a witch. It was perfect.

The mix of shock and smile on his face. She felt a flush of something... pride, maybe?

Then she ran as fast as she could.

The next year, she skipped trick-or-treating for a party at a friend's house. Instead of Dracula, she was stuck with Wade Barclay fumbling his way through the maze of her bra.

He got Seven Minutes in Heaven. She only got Second Base.

Neither of them wore a costume. Disappointing.

She never found out who'd been Dracula that first Halloween. She didn't really care. It had nothing to do with him, whoever he was. Besides, she knew it was wrong, knew she was supposed to tell. Grownups weren't supposed to feel up little girls. They weren't supposed to leave their teeth marks on their necks.

She figured he must still be out there. She wondered if he thought about her, wondered if he remembered her the way she remembered him... wondered if he still wore the teeth on Halloween.

Sometimes she wondered if he'd been caught, if he was in jail.

He should be.

She should have told someone.

She was sometimes tempted to ask one of her friends if they'd ever... but she didn't.

It wasn't about them. It wasn't about him.

It was her moment. That was enough.

Until now.

Tonight. She had it all planned.

This Halloween was her night to let it happen—or make it happen, if she had to.

Although, the way this night was going, it didn't look like much of anything was going to happen. She was seventeen. It was Halloween. She was ready to go all the way. And she was alone.

So, yeah, she was pissed off.

She walked toward the playground. She'd given up looking for Jimmy. She wasn't going to call his name. If he was going to play his little-kid games, then he was going to miss out. It was just his tough luck. It wasn't like she hadn't been dropping hints all fucking week, jokes about making sure he stocked up before the big night, about how she had a special treat for him. If he was too dumb to figure it out, then that was just tough shit for him.

There was always next year.

She stood for a moment in a patch of moonlight, turning in a circle and wondering where the hell he'd gone.

He was hiding. Probably planning to jump out and scare her. *Asshole.*

She wondered if maybe he might be… oh, she imagined him slipping a pair of fake teeth into his mouth and sliding up behind her, arm around her waist, fingers in her hair, his breath hot on the back of her neck.

Kelly stopped, held her breath.

Halloween… spooky old playground… maybe he wasn't so stupid after all, maybe he knew her better than she thought he did.

In a flash, all of her irritation tilted, folding over to reveal a burning need beneath. She licked her lips, bit the lower one until it stung… scanning the playground, wondering where he might be hiding.

The wind in the bare branches above. Rustle of leaves under her feet.

And, more and more, it looked like it might turn out to be his night, too.

She stepped over the low concrete ring bordering the playground, the spike heels of her boots driving into the soft sand.

She called out his name.

No answer.

There were three or four concrete tubes to one side. The light washed out the colors of the peeling paint, everything pale under the moon. Kelly approached the tubes and knelt down, peeking inside.

Empty.

She rocked for a moment on her heels, the edge of her lip between her teeth.

Familiar feeling—that soft pinch. She felt an echo of that ache within, tender flesh caught between teeth and fingertips…

Halloween. Her night.

The swings were empty, drifting in the October breeze. Ghosts.

Beyond, there were only trees and the shadows between them.

She straightened up, walking back to the edge of the sand. She stepped up onto the concrete ring and moved like an acrobat on a tightrope, tapping her heels on the ring as she walked along the perimeter toward the new jungle gym. It was way better than anything they had at her school when she'd been a kid. The tall platform was supported on all sides by clean wooden posts, with a long tubular slide curving down on itself as it reached the ground below.

From where she was standing, Kelly could see that the platform was empty. She wondered for a moment if maybe she was wrong, maybe he wasn't even here at all. Maybe he'd run on ahead, through the trees.

Maybe she was alone.

She climbed the ladder up to the platform and stood for a long moment, looking down over the sprawling playground.

Nothing, no sign of him.

"Jimmy?"

She waited for a moment. "I know you're here. If you don't show yourself by the time I get to the bottom of the slide, I'm leaving."

And you'll never get another chance, she didn't say. *At least, not until next year. Maybe not even then.*

She waited a moment more, then shrugged. "Okay…"

She pushed herself up on her palms, resting on top of the slide, suspended over the opening of the plastic tube.

And then she swung her feet forward, letting herself go… all the way down.

She screamed. There was something waiting there in the tube, something that rose up over her. She slid beneath the shadow and it fell down on her, all legs and arms, and something buried its head deep into the hollow of her neck and she felt the teeth, the heat of his breath just below her jaw and then it was her legs around him, holding him to her as they slid down the rest of the way and lay, intertwined, at the bottom edge of the slide.

Jimmy.

The fear, the press of him on her. She could feel his heat, the hard edge pushing back against her, his fingertips digging into her hair at the roots, his other hand… fingers tapping up the ladder of her ribs…

Fucking Halloween.

She heard herself whimper, dug her hands into the back pockets of his jeans, pulled him closer. He moaned when her fingernails dug into his buttocks, even through the denim she felt him twitch.

She was glad they hadn't done the whole costume thing this year. They didn't need it. She didn't need it.

It was Halloween. That was enough.

She smelled the bitter chemical tang of his cologne, chocolate on his breath. He was moving now, his hips… too fast and too soon. She wasn't ready for it to be over. It wasn't his night. It was hers.

She put her hands against his chest and rolled him over in the slide, pinning him for a moment as she straddled him, denim rough against the inside of her thighs, the metal rivets of his button-fly jeans like a spine against her. She longed to press harder.

And then she hopped off him, straightening her skirt. "You forgot to say Trick or Treat."

He lay there on the edge, half in and half out of the tube, his feet resting on the ground. She could not see his face in the shadows within, but Kelly could hear the echo of his breath.

She edged back to one side, knocked on the outside of the tube. "Anyone home?"

He did not answer, did not move.

She popped her head around the side, peeking in. "Trick or treat..?"

His hands shot out and Kelly let out a little scream, laughing as he pulled her back in on top of him.

She let him go a little bit further this time. She could feel Jimmy trying to sneak in around the edges of her defenses, fingertips tapping out a code on her nerve endings, looking for the password that would let him in. She laid her arms on top of the tube, turning her face up to the moon.

She let him explore as much as she wanted. Her legs trapped him there, holding him in place. She wouldn't let things go any further until she was ready.

But even that started to slip away from her, his momentum picking up... tapping, he almost broke the code.

Not yet. She hopped off, leaving him there in the tube. "No more candy. You'll spoil your dinner."

Jimmy didn't move.

She kicked his feet.

"Jesus!" He sat up, glared at her. "What'd you do that for?"

She laughed. "Just trying to get a rise out of you." She smirked. "Well, another one."

He stood up, untucked his shirt.

"So that's why you guys do that," she said. "Clever."

"Yeah." He dug his hands into his pockets.

Like that was going to help. She could see all of him there. His embarrassment might have been cute to some girls. Not to her. She didn't need it. "So... where is he?"

"Who?"

"Who." She snorted. "The kid. The ghost."

Jimmy shrugged, pretended to look around. "I don't know. Sometimes he doesn't show up."

"Uh huh." She narrowed her eyes. If he was bullshitting her, it was going to be a long, lonely walk back home. Just him and his boner. "'Sometimes he doesn't show up.'"

She went over to a wooden bench nearby and sat down. One of her boots had come untied and she took a moment to lace it up again. "If you were fucking lying…"

"…swear to god," he said. "I wasn't. He's really here."

"Better be."

Jimmy came over and sat down next to her on the bench. She shifted away from him a little bit, pretending to sulk. He leaned over to kiss her but she turned away.

"Fuck off."

"I love you." He sounded like he really meant it.

She felt a little sorry for him then, despite herself. It was Halloween. It was hers. It had nothing to do with him. But he didn't know that. "You're very sweet."

But the pout had already started. Even less attractive now. "Don't you love me?"

"I don't know." Kelly sighed. "But I want to fuck you, if that makes you feel any better."

A jumble of responses moved across his face. The flash of hurt and anger wiped away by confusion and shock, which in turn got pushed out of the way by someone not doing a very good job of hiding his big, stupid grin. "Really?"

Kelly would have called it off right there but she didn't want to wait another year. And he was cute, even if he wasn't smart enough to know how lucky he was.

But it was Halloween. She was ready.

She leaned into him, pulled herself around and swung her leg over his lap. His hands found their place at her waist, his hips adjusting slightly to fit better against her. Kelly's hands on his chest, tapping her thumbs against his sternum. The pagan beat of her heart, the gentle pulse of him between her thighs.

It was Halloween. She could taste the ghost of chocolate in his mouth, sweet and cheap. She was ready. She hoped it wouldn't be over too soon. She wanted it to be special, wanted it to last.

"Oh, baby…" he moaned, reaching up for her. "I want you."

No shit, Sherlock. She pushed his hands back down, rolling her eyes a little bit.

She leaned into him, letting herself go a little more. She didn't mind playing, teasing him along, teasing herself.

Then she opened her eyes and saw a little boy standing there, watching them.

"Jesus!" Kelly gasped, cold air filling her lungs. A coughing fit overtook her. She gasped again, almost choking.

"Oh god, baby…" Jimmy moaned in response, clueless as usual. He pulled her closer, wrapping his arms around her, sliding his hands up under her shirt.

Kelly saw the boy cock his head, his brow wrinkle.

"Fuck." She tried to roll off of Jimmy but he shifted his hips, grinding against her.

"Fuck me, baby…" he gasped.

She gagged, his candy breath rolling across her face.

Kelly tore herself free and jumped back, keeping the bench between her and the boy. "Get the fuck off me."

Jimmy stood up, confused. "What? What'd I do?"

"You… you fucking…" More coughing, she couldn't speak so she pointed.

He turned, saw the boy.

"Hi, Jimmy." The boy raised one hand, a feeble little wave.

"Hey." Jimmy adjusted his shirt, dug his hands into his pockets. "Sorry."

The boy frowned. "What were you doing?"

"Uh…"

"…is this him?" Kelly nudged past Jimmy.

He shot her a look.

"What?" She coughed again, trying to catch her breath. "Is it?"

Jimmy shrugged, put his hand on her shoulder. He smiled at the boy. "I brought someone to meet you. Okay?"

The boy looked at Jimmy for a long moment, barely acknowledging Kelly. He turned away from them and knelt in the sand. He began to dig.

"That's him?" Kelly grabbed Jimmy by the arm, whispered in his ear. "Is that him?"

"Yeah."

"He's just a kid," she hissed.

He nodded. "Yeah. I told you that."

"You told me he was…" Jimmy gave her a look. She dropped his arm and took a few steps toward the little boy.

"Kelly." Jimmy's voice, low.

She waved away the warning and stood watching the little boy, shaking her head. Annoyed again. That hard little knot inside.

Ignoring Jimmy's whispers, she went over and squatted down next to the boy. "Hey there…"

The boy did not look up.

"Whatcha doing, Caspar? You digging?"

"That's not my name."

Kelly rocked back on her heels. "Ooh, grumpiest ghost I know. Well, what is your name, then?"

The boy didn't answer.

Kelly picked a stick out of the sand and snapped it between her fingers. "What're you digging for, anyways? Treasure? Jewels, maybe?" She pretended to think for a moment. "Catshit..?"

Jimmy's hand on her shoulder. "Knock it off."

She shook him off, dropped her voice and whispered to the boy. "Bones?"

"Kelly." Jimmy didn't quite raise his voice.

She ignored him. Her eyes narrowed slightly, waiting.

The boy knelt there for a long moment, staring at the sand. He looked up to Jimmy, his face flat and pale in the moonlight.

Then he stood up and turned away, heading for the trees.

"Hey," Kelly grabbed the boy's arm. "Where you going?"

The boy froze. Slowly, he turned his head to stare at her.

Kelly grabbed his hand in both of hers, frowned. "Your hand's warm."

"So is yours," the boy replied.

"You're just a kid." She glared back over her shoulder at Jimmy. "He's just, he's only a kid."

Jimmy nodded. "Yeah. I told you he…"

"…shut the fuck up." She gripped the little boy's wrists, digging her nails in. "You're just a kid?"

The boy winced. "Please let go of…"

But she cut him off, hissing back over her shoulder at Jimmy. "You told me he…"

She turned on the boy once more. "You know what he told me? Do you?"

"Let go," the boy said, his voice cracking around the edges. "Please don't."

"Kelly…" Jimmy grabbed her shoulder.

"You know what he said you were?" Kelly shook the boy's arm. "Do you?"

Jimmy tried to pull her away. "Come on, you said you'd be cool."

"Be cool?" She shook the boy again. "You know what he told me?"

"I know…" the boy said.

"You little shit." Kelly yanked the boy toward her, holding his chin between her thumb and forefinger. "Who are you? What's your name?"

The boy shook his head, starting to cry now.

She narrowed her eyes. "I want to hear you say it."

"Yes." He was sobbing.

"Little. Shit." She shook him again. Punctuation.

"Hey!" Jimmy grabbed her shoulder. "Leave him alone."

Kelly turned on him, dragging the little boy around with her. Jimmy stood uncertain, utterly worthless.

"You know, you drag me out here for…" Kelly shook her head. "It's fucking Halloween and you wasted the whole fucking night…"

Her jaw snapped shut on the words. She glared at Jimmy. "I let you fucking rub all over me, turns out it's just a bullshit fucking kid?"

She thrust the boy forward at Jimmy. "Who is he?"

Jimmy didn't answer. She dragged the boy back to face her. "What's your name? Tell me!"

Jimmy saw something pass over the little boy's face. There was a momentary flicker of… what?

The boy shifted in her grasp and suddenly straightened out his arm, shoving Kelly off balance.

He had hold of her hand now.

So strong. Kelly felt a sudden flush of cold.

"Your name, your name, your name…" He locked eyes with her, wiping his nose with his free hand. His voice was low, soft… growing louder.

"Your name is Kelly… Kelly Green."

Kelly felt a tremor move over her, flickering across her shoulder blades like a snake. She shivered, trying to free her hand.

"Kelly Green," the boy said again. "That's your name and you, and you, and you hate it. You hate your name."

"I…" Kelly couldn't speak. The boy's voice rolled over her, crushing the breath from her lungs.

"Kelly Green. You hate it, you hate it because it's your name and because it's a color…"

"…what did you say?" Kelly gasped. She could feel her eyes widening, her mouth opening. She didn't understand how this kid knew…

"…it's a color." The boy's voice cut through the chill air between them. "And your mother, your mother, your mother, she used to, she always made you wear…"

Oh, no no no… Kelly thought to herself. *No way.*

"She made you wear it all the, all the time when you were, when you were little."

There was something new in his voice. Was it pity? "Kelly Green in kelly green."

"Stop it." Jimmy knew this was his fault. But he could only stand and watch.

But the boy in the red sweater wasn't done yet. "And when, and when you were little…"

"…please, please stop." Kelly was crying now, kneeling in front of the boy.

"When you were little, you, you, someone bad…" The boy's face collapsed into itself for a split second, as though he might break down sobbing as well. But then it smoothed out once more, placid like the moon. "Something, someone bad, something bad happened to you and now you, now you don't love, you can't love anyone and you won't, you never, you never will…"

"…oh fuck, oh god…"

"…but sometimes, sometimes, you think, you think about it, you want to, you think about making yourself dead…"

"…Jesus." Kelly reached back with her free hand, toward Jimmy. "Help me…"

But Jimmy didn't, couldn't, move.

The boy's words came now all in a rush, as though he had to get it all out, fast as he could. "You're pretty and you're happy now, Kelly Green, but in, but in, but in, in one-two-three-four-five-six-seven-eight-nine-ten, in ten years, in ten years you're going to wake up, you'll get up every day, every day, and you'll go, you'll go to the mirror, scared, scared, scared of what you're going to see, scared of who will, who will be looking back at you..."

"...please." Pleading like a little girl, Kelly could hear it in her voice and she couldn't help herself. She felt the press of her bladder, insistent, suddenly full.

"But you don't need, you don't need, don't need to worry because, because, because you'll never grow old, Kelly, Kelly Green..."

"...stop it." Jimmy finally found his voice, took a step toward the boy.

But the boy wasn't finished. "You'll never get old."

He dropped Kelly's hand and backed away, very small.

Kelly slumped backward at Jimmy's feet, sobbing. He helped her stand up.

The boy in the red sweater stood looking at them, tears streaming down his cheeks. "I'm sorry."

Jimmy held Kelly, her body shuddering as the sobs ran through her.

"Jimmy..." The boy took a step toward them.

Jimmy shook his head. "Go away."

The boy's face twisted, remorse and grief mingling. "I'm sorry..."

"...just go."

"I'm sorry..." Almost a wail now.

"I know." Jimmy nodded. He could feel his face smoothing out into a mask, doing his best not to lose it. Kelly pressing on him. He couldn't help thinking that he might have another chance with her. "Just... just go, all right? Please."

The boy twisted his fingers together, his mouth working. "Are you mad at..?"

"...it's all right. Just go." Clipped, final. "Please."

The boy in the red sweater stood for a moment longer. Jimmy

thought that he might try to say something else, maybe reach out and try to comfort the girl too. Jimmy didn't think she could take it. He had a mental image of Kelly flying apart when the boy touched her, spinning away in the wind.

He honestly didn't know how much longer he could stand the boy's presence, the creeping chill that had been running up and down his back since the boy first spoke to Kelly. If he had known what the boy could do…

After a long moment, the boy ran off through the swings, sending them bouncing as he passed, the clatter of the chains dull in the cold air.

Jimmy watched him go, a mix of anger and relief. He had the sudden impulse to leave Kelly behind and follow the boy. He had so many more questions now, but… Kelly.

She shuddered again, turned her head to the side and laid her face against his chest.

Jimmy felt very grown-up all of a sudden.

"Oh god…"

He winced at her breath, soured with fear.

"It's all right," he told her.

"Is he..?" She raised her head. "Did he..?"

"…he's gone." The mask was still in place. Jimmy was angry with her, but she was so warm against him.

She started to cry again. "What is this? What is this?"

He searched for something he could say to undo all of the damage he'd done, something to let everyone off the hook for this stupid idea.

"It was just…" He cleared his throat, the words not quite there. "It was just a trick."

Kelly raised her face to look at him. Her makeup had gone to pieces under the flow of tears, a smeared mask.

Just like mine. He cleared his throat again.

"A trick?" Confusion, disbelief... then a flicker of anger flared to life, consuming her entire face. "You what..?"

She pulled back from him, broke his grip. "You fucking asshole!"

Kelly lunged for Jimmy, landing a few fairly solid smacks against his chest before he grabbed her wrists. "Fucking let go of me!"

He was talking very fast now, almost shaking her in time to the rhythm of his words. "It's all right, it's all right... it was just, it was just a trick... just a trick, we were just trying to scare you, it's Halloween, it was just a kid, just a kid from the neighborhood..."

One hand got free, found his cheek. A rake. "Fucker!"

He grabbed for her again, trying to dodge her flailing hands. "I'm sorry, I'm so sorry, Kelly..."

She slumped against him, sobbing once more.

Finally she managed to choke out "Was it, was... it was just a trick?"

Jimmy nodded. "Yeah, I just... I didn't mean to, we just wanted to scare you and I thought..."

He pretended to search for words. "I know you like Halloween."

"Oh god, just shut up..." Kelly pulled his face down to hers, closing off his words with a quiet, hungry moan.

He let her, feeling her relief, knowing she was choosing this, choosing to believe his hasty lie over the truth, choosing the easier thing, the sane thing that wouldn't destroy her mind.

And he let her.

They fumbled their way to the ground, comforting each other with all the lies their bodies could tell... until even that ended and they fell silent under the skeletal branches, the darkness beyond.

WINTER

Jim watched his son float away, then return.

The swingset chains squealed in the chill air. It had not snowed yet. But winter was here.

The playground was a shambles. The place he'd played as a boy had grown shabby over the years, splintering around the edges.

As he'd gotten older, someone—a group of concerned neighbors maybe?—had gone out of their way to replace all of the old, sturdy-but-rusty playground toys with newer, shiny models made from molded plastic and recycled tires.

They'd done their best, a new plastic world superimposed over the top of his memories.

Plastic. So easy to scrape and carve with a keychain, burn with cigarettes, or splinter under insistent adolescent rage.

And so, what had stood the test of time for decades—albeit a little rusty around the edges—was reduced to wreckage within a few years.

Because memories last. Like wood, they can decay… but we're careful with them because they were once alive. Not so much with plastic.

A few of the older things had been left behind. Nostalgia or because the money ran out. Broken boards, splintered fiberglass and plastic, rusted metal and crumbling concrete, faded and peeling paint, a sandbox littered with broken bottles and trash. It was not a safe place for children, not anymore.

If it ever was... Jim thought to himself, pushing James on the swing. He could feel how thin and light his son had become. Even bundled up in his puffy coat, scarf, hat, mittens... even so, his son felt hollow under his hands.

Jim had dreamed last night that he was out walking with his son and the wind came up...

...the wind came up, whipping past them, they could see it coming, gathering up little cyclones of dried leaves and dust, moving from one side of the street to the other, Jim saw it coming along the sidewalk opposite them, there was no time to run, the cyclone turned and crossed the road, heading straight for them, there was no time to run, so Jim knelt down and threw his arms around his son, covering him...

...it whipped over them, his eyes and mouth full of dust...

...and then it was gone...

...and he woke up to nothing—his arms empty, the lingering sorrow, his son borne away in the teeth of the wind.

Lost in his thoughts, he'd forgotten to keep pushing. His son had come to a gentle stop and they waited there in the still, cold air together. For a moment, the knot in Jim's throat was too much for him. He prayed that the boy would not turn around, would not see it all there on his face.

Jim pushed the knot down, did his best to smooth over his face so his son wouldn't know. He had made a decision long ago not to let self-pity or sorrow eclipse their time together. So far, he'd failed miserably. But he was still trying.

"We should probably get going soon, buddy." It was getting late, getting cold. "Be dark soon."

"What?" The boy in the swing tilted his head to one side and pushed the thick earflap out of the way so he could hear.

Jim's throat closed again at the sight of the pale, bare scalp. "We need to start heading back," he managed.

"Not yet."

"It's…" Jim cleared his throat. "It's pretty cold."

"Not yet." James let the ear flap fall again.

It was getting more and more difficult for Jim to say no to the boy. The kid was getting older, getting smarter every day. And, in their situation, the normal rules and responsibilities didn't seem to apply anymore.

Unfortunately, James' mom didn't agree.

Jim tapped a little tune on the boy's shoulders with his gloved fingertips. "Your mom'll be looking for us. She'll get mad if I let you freeze into a popsicle."

James wiped his nose, drawing a faint silvered snail track across the back of his mitten. "I won't freeze."

"You might." Jim stamped his feet to get the blood flowing. "Big ol' popsicle kid sitting on the couch watching cartoons."

James made a noise, scornful.

But Jim could hear the smile on the boy's face, even if he couldn't see it. "Yeah, freeze you right up like Walt Disney."

"Who?"

"Disneyland?" Jim didn't think he'd done that bad a job as a dad. "Guy who invented Mickey Mouse?"

James half-turned in the swing to look back at his father. "He froze?"

Jim shrugged. "Some people say that before he died, he had his doctors freeze him."

"Really?" The boy's pale face was so thin, Jim could almost read his thoughts through the skin. "Why?"

"He wanted to…" Jim stopped, started again. "He thought that one day they would be able to thaw him out and wake him up and make him better, once science had caught up."

James' pale green eyes found those of his father. "He was sick?"

Jim nodded. "Uh huh."

"With what?" The boy had a lot of interest in illness and medicine now. He might grow up to be a doctor, if he didn't…

Jim pushed the thought out of his mind.

"He had cancer." The matter-of-fact mask slipped into place. Jim barely thought of it anymore. Just another way to make things easier for both of them.

"Did it work?" There was a flicker in the boy's eyes—a brief glimmer of hope fluttering against the fatigue.

Jim knew it well. He loved to see it. A little ember in the snow.

"Well, last I heard, he was still dead. So probably not." He knew a laugh was too much to expect, but he'd at least hoped for a smile.

He got neither.

"But would it work?"

"I don't think so." Jim came around to the front of the swings. "And besides, if you did get frozen and woken up later, everyone you knew would be dead."

The conversation had taken a darker turn into territory Jim wanted to avoid.

Too late.

"Everything would be different," he told the boy. "Everyone would be gone. You wouldn't know anyone anymore. You'd be all alone."

"Like a ghost," the boy replied.

"Yeah." Jim touched his chin, holding the mask in place. "Except you'd still be alive."

"I might be lonely," James agreed. "But at least I wouldn't be sick anymore."

Jim nodded. "No. Not anymore."

The boy twisted back and forth on the swing, his face tilted to the sky. "It's cold."

He pushed off with his toes, letting his shoes drag in the near-frozen sand.

Jim had a desperate need to scoop up the boy in his arms, crush him close. But he did not know if he could bear to feel the fragile weight of his son in his arms. "You okay?"

The boy shrugged. "Just thinking."

"What're you thinking about?"

James shrugged again. "Just thinking."

Jim watched his son for a long moment, then asked again because he couldn't help himself. "You okay?"

James looked up. "Yeah."

Jim nodded and stepped away, fumbling in his pockets. He pulled out a battered pack of cigarettes, tapped one out, lit it.

He exhaled shadow into the air.

"I thought you quit." His son was looking at him, lips pressed together to hold in the disappointment.

Just like your mother. "So did I."

"It's bad for you."

"Yeah." Jim shrugged. "Yes. It is."

"You'll get cancer and we'll have to freeze you like Walt Disney."

"Who?"

"Guy who made up Mickey Mouse."

"Oh, yeah," Jim said slowly. "Him."

But James wasn't letting him off the hook. "Mom quit." He hopped off of the swing and headed for the slide.

His father followed. "Good for mom."

Jim held his breath while his son climbed the ladder. "Careful up there."

"I'm all right."

"Yeah, well, be careful anyway."

The boy looked down at him, rocked back and forth. A taunt.

"We really should get back."

James stood for a long moment on the platform at the top of the slide, looking out over the playground. "What about your friend?"

Good question. "I don't, I don't think he comes here to play anymore."

"Maybe he got tired of waiting."

"Maybe." Jim hadn't told James anything, not really. Just that they were going to meet a little kid he knew.

But still... Jim was worried. He'd made this mistake before. More than once.

He couldn't help it. This was his son.

James said "Maybe he's just late. Maybe he got lost."

"Maybe."

"Maybe... maybe his car broke down."

Jim picked up the thread. "And maybe... he had to walk to find a telephone."

"Yeah, and maybe..." James thought for a moment. "And maybe he got lost and fell into a hole."

"And maybe... snow covered him up and he froze, just like Walt Disney."

"Who?"

Jim smiled. "Guy who built Disneyland."

James nodded. "Oh, yeah. Him."

"Don't mock me, shorty."

James cocked his head. "What's 'mock' mean?"

"It means..." Jim thought for a moment. "It means 'make fun of.'"

James nodded. "Oh. Yeah."

"'Oh. Yeah.'"

"Don't mock me."

Jim smiled. There was nothing better than this: Just him and his son, together. Tossing words back and forth like a game of catch. "Come on, let's head back."

"Not yet." James looked out over the playground.

Jim couldn't help but wonder what he was thinking. There was so much happening, all at once. The boy couldn't possibly take it all in, sort through all of the emotions. And yet, here he was—calmly looking out over a playground, as smooth and placid as a Zen monk.

Then James spoke, breaking the silence. "How old is he?"

Jim frowned, confused for a moment. "Walt Disney?"

The boy shook his head. "Your friend."

"Ah. Good question." He nodded, buying some time and not entirely sure what he should say, how much he should say. "Honestly? I have no idea."

"When's his birthday?"

Jim shrugged. "I don't know."

"Is he older than me?"

"Yes." Well, that wasn't not quite right. "No. Sort of… he's just a kid."

That was safe. That was true. Mostly.

He walked around the jungle gym, stopping at the foot of the slide. The tube was decorated with crude scrawls—wannabe gang tags and cartoon pornography almost clinical in its anatomical accuracy. Pre-pubescent cave paintings to the gods of lust and war.

The green plastic had worn through in spots, splintering along the seams as it aged. Jim ran his fingertips over the rough edges, careful not to snag on the curled shards.

His son called down from above. "What'cha doing?"

"Thinking."

"What'cha thinking?"

Jim held his hands out, palms turned up to the gray sky. "I don't know. I was thinking about someone I used to know. Long time ago."

The boy narrowed his eyes. "Who?"

"Just…" Jim shook his head. "Just an old friend."

"Your girlfriend?"

Jim shook his head. "A girlfriend. From a long time ago. Before I knew your mom. When I was in high school."

"What was her name?"

"Doesn't matter."

James scratched his chin, eyes still on his father, doing his best to be nonchalant. "Is she still your girlfriend?"

"No." Jim looked up sharply, his own eyes narrowing. "I don't have a girlfriend."

"Mom says you do."

Bitch. "Well, your mom can…"

He took a breath, held it for a long while. "Listen. Your mom is mad at me. You know that."

"Yeah."

"And she…" Jim had already given up trying to explain to everyone all of the reasons why. Everyone was so surprised by the divorce, like they had no idea that such a thing was possible. He'd spent hours saying the same thing over and over, answering all the questions from family and friends.

And, with each telling, he shifted from anger to irritation to, eventually, just plain boredom.

All that effort and for what? Few of them understood—or wanted to understand—so he just gave up trying altogether.

Except with James. He promised himself that he wouldn't hide anything from his son, that he'd never lie, and answer any question as best he could.

He took another breath, let it out in a plume of heat and fog in the cold air. "She doesn't understand. Your mom thinks…" He looked up.

His son was watching, looking down on him.

Jim circled the jungle gym once more, counterclockwise.

"Listen buddy, I won't lie to you. Things happen to people. They change. You start off one way and then somehow you end up a completely different person. It's not your fault, it's not anything you did. But it happened and, well, it happens to everyone all the time. Sometimes, if you're married, you change together… and sometimes you change in different ways, different from each other."

He broke off. He hated that careful balance, telling the truth but not telling more than the boy needed to hear.

"When you're married—listen, you don't need to worry about this, about any of this, not right now. Not for a long time."

"How long?"

"I don't know."

Jim tried to smile, to pass it off as no big deal. "Twenty years."

James shook his head. "How long?"

"A long time." Jim wanted to climb up, to squat down and grab the boy by the shoulders, look at him eye-to-eye. "Don't worry about it. A lot happens between now and then."

"Like what?"

"A lot." Jim put some weight into that last word, heavy enough to give James something strong enough to stand on. A foundation.

"Like what?"

Jim took a long breath, let it all out—shadows in the cold air.

"You grow up. You lose all your teeth and get new ones. You make friends who move away. You learn to whistle and pop wheelies on your bike. You go to school, make friends. Then you go to high school, and change your friends. You start smoking. You drink your first beer."

Jim smiled to himself. "Sometimes not in that order. You fall in love. You get your heart broken. You do it all over again. And then again."

Jim kept walking, circling. His son above, looking down. "You get a job. You get married. You get gray hair. You make friends. You move away. You move back. You have kids. You quit smoking. Your kids get bigger. Your heart gets broken again. You change jobs, change haircuts, change friends. You start smoking again. You go bald…"

He stopped his circle around the jungle gym and raised his hands, palms up… then let them fall. "And all of it… it all changes you, little by little, until…"

Jim looked up. His son was standing at the top of the slide, eyes closed, his face raised to the pale sky. The boy was weaving slightly on his feet.

"What's wrong?" Jim felt his heart skip a bit. He had a sudden flash, his son letting go and tumbling away on the wind.

"James? You okay?" His voice sharp in the chill air.

"Yes." The boy did not open his eyes.

"Are you okay?" James tensed, ready to spring forward. He would not let his son fall.

"I am okay."

When he was younger, James would sometimes talk in his sleep. His voice would drift across the hall to where his father and mother slept. Jim would rise at the first murmur and go to his son, sitting on the edge of the boy's bed, listening to his son's voice until the tide rose and carried the boy back off into the deeper waters of sleep once more.

That was how James sounded now. Dreaming awake.

He looks so tired, Jim thought. *He looks so old.*

"What are you doing?"

"I'm smelling."

The annnoyance in the boy's voice was reassuring. It grounded him, somehow. "The playground smells different at night."

Jim nodded. "That's winter, the snow. A cold snap. You can smell it coming."

"What's a cold snap?"

"It's a…"

But the boy interrupted him. "It is cold, you're right. I can smell it. The cold."

"Maybe it's this?" Jim held up his dead cigarette.

The boy shook his head. "It's not cigarettes, dad. It's winter."

"Oh."

His son looked at him with such disappointment. "You should quit."

Jim shrugged, weakly. "Yeah."

"They're bad for you," his son told him for the hundredth time.

"That's what I hear." Jim cocked an eyebrow, considered lighting another one but decided against it. James wouldn't think it was funny.

"You could get that gum…"

"…come on." James flicked the butt away, motioning to the boy. "Let's go back, make some hot chocolate."

James considered this. "The real or the powder?"

"Real." Recently James had become a connoisseur. Jim was not above using this as leverage. "Promise?"

"Yes."

"Where'd you get it?"

"I bought it."

"Where'd you buy it?"

"From a store."

"Where'd they get it?"

"They bought it."

"Where'd they buy it?"

The trick was to go fast, to answer before the other person had a chance to think, throw them off guard, make them fumble or hesitate. Whoever dropped the ball, lost.

"From a farmer."

"Where did he get it?"

"From a cow."

"Cows don't make chocolate."

"From a chocolate cow."

"There's no such thing as a chocolate cow."

"Who says?"

"I say."

"How do you know?"

"I just know."

"There isn't?"

"No."

"You sure?"

"You know there isn't."

"Maybe. But I wish there was."

"Maybe it'll come true because you wished it."

"My wishes don't come true."

"Like me getting better?"

Jim dropped the ball. It lay there for a long time between them, gray and heavy as the world.

He did not look up at his son. "Like that, yeah."

They stood there in the cold. Lost.

But at least they were together.

"I might, you know," James said quietly.

Jim nodded. "I know."

"Do you think I will?"

"I don't know." Jim tried very, very hard not to look like he was hunting for the right thing to say. "I want you to."

"But do you wish for it?"

Oh God…

"Every day." Jim honestly didn't know how long he could keep it up, this mask. Every day it splintered around the edges a little bit more.

"It might happen." There was no hope in the boy's voice, no attempt to comfort himself or his father. He merely spoke a fact, like someone commenting on the weather but accepting whatever came.

"It might…" Without thinking, Jim fumbled another cigarette out of the pack and began to light it before… he looked up guiltily at the boy.

"You're going to die before me," his son said. "If you don't quit."

Jim tossed the cigarette away, unlit. "Come on down."

"I don't want to go yet."

"I want you to meet someone."

There was a boy, James saw, standing off to one side near his father.

James coughed, then again—his throat, very dry.

"Come on down," his dad told him. "Come say hi."

James hopped into the slide, nearly knocking his father over at the bottom.

"Jeez," his dad said, sounding very much like a kid himself.

"Sorry."

"It's okay. Be careful, though."

James stood, brushing off the seat of his pants. The little boy waited a few feet away, scared or maybe shy. The boy had his hands shoved into the pockets of his jeans, shoulders hunched inside his red sweater.

James felt his dad's hand on his shoulder. "Son, this is my friend. The one I was telling you about."

James nodded. "Hi."

The boy nodded back.

"This is my son. This is James."

"Hello." The boy said.

"Uh… hi." James said again. He looked up at his father but his dad was focused on the other boy.

"I wasn't sure you'd still be here." His dad's face was unreadable.

The boy in the red sweater didn't answer.

There was something in his dad's voice, James could hear it. Like he was apologizing for something. "Are you still digging?"

The boy nodded. "Yes."

"I thought maybe you'd found...'

"...dad?" James motioned and his father bent down. James whispered something.

His dad stood up again. "Why don't you ask him yourself?"

James shook his head. He felt like a little kid, first day of school—not knowing anyone, forced to make friends.

His dad sighed, turned to the boy in the red sweater. "He wants to know, aren't you cold?"

"No."

James pulled his dad down, whispering again.

"Ask him yourself, you want to know."

James looked at the boy, then back to his dad.

After a long moment, his dad chuckled. "He wants to know your name."

The boy in the red sweater took a breath but before he could speak, his face clouded over. He turned as a wash of light spilled over the three of them standing there in the playground, spreading out their shadows, long like sundials moving across the pale face of the day.

James heard a car door slam, the familiar hum of an engine.

His mother's voice: "James..."

He could hear her trudging through the sand.

"It's mom," he told his dad.

"I know." His dad did not turn around.

James looked in the direction his father was watching.

The other boy was gone.

And then his mom was there in the beam of her headlights, all frustration and noise. She looked tired, pained. James couldn't remember a time when her face didn't look like that. "Hi mom."

She gave him a tight crease of a smile, her eyes on his father. "Go get in the car. It's cold."

"Mom…" James knew where this was headed.

"James." That one word, her voice, was enough.

"Sorry." James looked up and saw the same apology in his dad's eyes.

"Go on, buddy." His dad smiled, letting both of them off the hook. "Here, give me a hug first."

He knelt down and James let himself be embraced.

After a long moment the boy pulled back and pushed his dad's knit cap up off his forehead, exposing the shaved head underneath.

"What're you doing?" his dad asked.

James pulled off his right mitten and, traced something on his dad's forehead with his forefinger.

"What are you doing?" Jim asked again.

James stepped back and looked at his father's face for a moment.

He leaned in close, whispering.

Closing his eyes, Jim nodded.

And then his son was running through the light to the warmth of his mother's car.

Jim watched him go.

Once the car door slammed, Jim stood up and occupied himself with brushing sand off his jeans. He did his best not to look at his ex-wife.

Joyce had a particular skill at making her displeasure clear, obvious. It was in the air all around her, like snow flurries. Soon enough, it would pile up all around them. And then Jim would have to shovel his way out. Again.

"Uh, what the hell is wrong with you?" It was a common question. Jim had long since given up on trying to answer it. "You can't drag him out here in the middle of winter."

"I didn't drag…" Jim took a breath, reminding himself yet again not to take the bait. "He wanted to come."

"He's sick." She swung it at him like a lash… A well-practiced hand.

"He wanted to."

"Do you do everything he wants?"

"Yes. I do." He took out his cigarettes, fitted one into the corner of his mouth and lit it.

The car horn honked once, then again.

Joyce squinted back into the headlights. "What's he doing?"

Jim slid his cap back on. He saw her eyes narrow as she turned back. "And what happened to your hair?"

"Got a haircut."

"Is this some kind of sick joke? You think this is funny?"

"No," Jim said. "I do not think this is funny."

"How do you think this makes him feel, this sick little joke of yours?"

Sick little..?

Deep breath. Then another. "He went with me."

"What?" She stared at him. "Why?"

Jim couldn't help it, he had to try to explain. "The other kids at school, some of them were making fun of him. Because of his hair. It's been going on for a while now, in case you didn't know. So I went to pick him up early and we went over to Jerry's. I told him 'If they make fun of you, they'll have to make fun of me, too.' So we went back, just after school. I stood outside with him, our caps in our hands. And we looked every single one of those little fuckers right in the eye. Not one of them laughed. Not today. And I bet they won't tomorrow, either."

He flicked his cigarette away, the sparks disappearing into the dark.

"You picked him up early?" Joyce sputtered like a match in the wind. "Who..? You, you took him out of school without my permission?"

"You're missing the point." Jim was already regretting that he'd bothered.

"The point, Jim, is that he's in school." Her chin went out, a dagger thrust. "You don't drag him out to..."

"...I didn't drag him..."

"…no, no, no. No." She held up her hand, shaking her head with her eyes closed. "You don't get to do that shit anymore. This won't, I'm calling Donna's office first thing on Monday morning and…"

"…fine, go right ahead." *Should have known better,* Jim told himself. "Give her a call. Waste more money."

He lit another cigarette, resisting the urge to blow smoke in her face.

The car horn honked again.

Joyce looked back. "What the hell is he doing?"

Jim held the cigarette up. "He wants me to put this out."

She crossed her arms. "You should."

"Mm."

"I quit."

Nothing more judgmental than a reformed smoker. "Good for you."

"You should too."

Jim shrugged. "Yeah, well, that's what it says on the pack."

She moved in for the kill. "You shouldn't smoke around James. It's bad for him."

"What, is he going to get more cancer?"

Jim took a small degree of pride, however perverse, in this rejoinder. He'd been rehearsing it for weeks.

Joyce's hands fluttered up to her mouth, a perfect parody of maternal shock and horror. She'd been rehearsing her own outrage for years. Jim had season tickets.

"You know…" She shook her head. "Sometimes I wonder how you get through life."

"You and me both."

"Why did you do this to us, to him?"

Inwardly, Jim rolled his eyes. She'd called dibs a long time ago when he filed for divorce: She got to be the victim and he was cast as the villain.

Jim was fine with that, so long as James knew the truth.

She narrowed her eyes. "There's something wrong with you, something broken. You're ill. You're sick. Mentally."

"Hey, y'know… everybody's gotta have a hobby."

"I never should have given you custody."

Given?

At this, Jim's anger flared to life. He couldn't help it. "You didn't have anything to say about it. And thank God for that, otherwise James wouldn't have anyone to hold him up and show him how to have some grace and defiance in the face of this fucking thing that's eating away at him."

"Uh, grace?" She rolled her eyes. "You call shaving your head grace?"

"No." Jim shook his head. "I call it defiance."

"Big man. Facing down a bunch of kids on the playground. So tough."

"Yeah, well, I'm pretty sure they won't make fun of him anymore."

Joyce sat down on the bench, resting her forehead in her upturned hand. She looked wrung out, like an old rag.

Jim resisted the urge to feel sorry for her.

"I don't understand you." Her voice was low, there were tears somewhere in there, circling around the edges. "I don't understand any of this."

"Any of what?" Jim knew all these lines. They'd rehearsed them so many times before.

She lifted her head to look at him. The raw, freshly-cut hate that only the blades of divorce can cultivate was sharp and sour. Evergreen. "I don't understand anything you do. I don't understand why, why did you do this to yourself? Why did you do this to us?"

"Are we still talking about my haircut?" Jim was so tired of all of this. He wanted to fall over and let the snow cover him up forever.

"Why are you doing this to me?"

Jim's breath, cold fog. "I'm not doing anything to you."

"How can you do this to your son? He needs you."

Jim felt his jaw clench. "He has me."

"Yeah." She opened her eyes. "Every other weekend."

Jim did his best not to take the bait. Failed. "And who chose that?"

"You left." Joyce slapped her hand down on the bench, the sound dead in the chill air. "Don't you feel bad about that? Don't you? Not even for him?"

"Some, yeah." Jim looked past her, toward the headlights. He could not see his son. "Yes. A little bit."

He heard the car door slam, feet running toward them.

Joyce glared at him. "You bastard."

"Don't you call me…"

But James had reached them. "Dad?"

The boy waited, just at the edge of the minefield.

"Yeah buddy?"

"Get back in the car, James." Joyce didn't turn, didn't look at her son… her eyes cold, only on Jim.

James shook his head. "I wanted to…"

"…go back and get warm." Joyce's anger was starting to shift, to focus on the boy.

"I want to ask dad something."

Jim knelt down as his son came to him. "Hey buddy? Listen to your mom."

"Dad…"

"…you go back in the car where it's warm, okay?"

"But I forgot to ask you, can you come on Tuesday?"

Jim nodded, doing his best to try and remember what the hell was happening Tuesday. "You bet. Count on it."

"James." Joyce was getting more and more brittle every moment.

"Wait mom, because…"

"…don't worry." Jim knew it was going to snap, Joyce's temper.

Shards everywhere. He didn't want James to have to endure any of that on his account.

"Because it's the last one." James' eyes flickered back and forth between his parents.

"I know." Jim remembered. *Fucking chemo. Poison for poison. The cure's worse than the disease. Just like life.*

"I'll be there."

The boy gave himself—gave all three of them, really—a quick flash of what could not be called hope but, at best, optimism. "And then maybe I'll be all done."

"Yeah," Jim agreed. "That'll be a good thing."

James shrugged. "Or… unless I have to do it again."

"Jim." Joyce stood up, looked pointedly at Jim over the boy's head.

Jim ignored her. "I know, buddy. Let's hope for all done. You're getting tired though, I can tell." The boy's eyes were hollow pits of shadow in the dim light.

Almost a skull. Jim pushed the thought from his mind. "Go back to the car and let me and mom finish up. Okay?"

"Okay."

"Okay." Jim gave him a big, fake smile.

His son knew it. James tapped his father's forehead. "Don't forget."

Jim nodded. "I won't. I don't."

James moved back into the lights and headed to the car.

His mother and father watched him go.

Joyce turned to Jim. "Don't forget what?"

Jim stared at her, a blank mask. He didn't want to share anything with her.

"What did he tell you not to forget?"

"What he said before."

"What did he say?"

Jim didn't want to tell her. It wasn't hers. James had given it to him.

Jim sighed. "He said 'I wrote my name on you.'"

"I don't understand what that means."

Jim was disappointed, but not surprised. Against his better judgment and previous experience, he couldn't help but try one more time to explain something to her.

"See," he said. "That's grace. I don't know a grownup who has an ounce of the strength and grace that kid has. That's what will get him through this."

A pitying look. "Jim. He's not going to 'get through' anything. He's dying."

Jim's rage was cold. Immense. He could barely contain it. "You don't know that."

Her face clenched, so like a fist. "He's not getting better. He won't feel this good for much longer, if ever again. No matter what you think. A few weeks maybe, if he's lucky. And then it'll go to shit again."

"Well, isn't it lucky that his mom hasn't given up on him yet."

She said nothing.

Jim swallowed, his throat tight. "He might. He might make it through. It's happened before."

"Two remissions. One. Two." Joyce ticked the false hopes off on her fingers. "Two of them. God knows how many surgeries and appointments... And now it's back. Again. He's spent more of his life sick than well."

She shook her head. "I don't know that I want him to make it through. Don't you remember last time, waiting? Watching him every day? Wanting to hope but being afraid? Knowing that he knew? Knowing that he could feel it before we could see it... feeling it creeping back in from wherever it had been hiding. Do you want to put him through that again?"

Jim said nothing.

She sighed. "I don't. I won't."

They were at the heart of it now. "You want him to die."

"Uh, if it's that or watch him live in pain and torture?" Joyce looked at him like he was an idiot. "Then yeah, I want him to be at peace."

Peace. Jim was very tired—tired of this argument, tired of her presence and all of the noise it brought, tired of feeling so sad.

"Who says you're at peace when you die?"

"At least it'll be over."

Jim shook his head. "Nothing's ever over."

"Except for us." She clearly thought she'd scored a point.

Jim said nothing. It just wasn't worth it.

"Why are you doing this?" Joyce asked him, yet again.

Fine. One last try…

"You gave up."

Her brow clenched with irritation. "I never gave up. I would have done anything to save this marriage."

"No." Jim pointed to the headlights. "You gave up on him. You gave up on James."

"I didn't…"

"…you did. You said it yourself, you want him to die."

Jim took a long breath, held it for a moment. "And he knows it."

She sat there, nothing but hate in her. "I want you to die."

And with that, she headed back to her car.

Jim saw a brief flash of his son's face as the overhead light came on when she opened the car door. The shadow of the boy's hand waving after it went off again.

The headlights swept past him and turned away, trailing anger red and white in their wake.

It was dark, Jim realized. Night had fallen and the streetlights were far enough away to do little good lighting the playground.

He stood for a long moment, eyes closed.

"Are you there?"

There was no answer. He let out a long breath.

Jim went to the bench and sat down, leaning back to stare up at the crisp winter stars above.

"Are you there? Are you?"

Nothing but the ache in his ears from the cold.

"I… listen to me. I'd like to…" A crack in his voice betrayed him, thin ice and nothing but cold sorrow beneath.

"Are you there?"

No answer.

"Because I need to know if… listen to me, I don't know if you're listening, but I want to know about my son. The boy you met?" Jim could hear the desperation in his voice, his brittle words.

"He's sick. It isn't, he isn't doing well and…" He faltered again. This all led to insanity, he knew. Sitting in the dark, talking to ghosts.

The only thing that matters is James.

"I know you know things, I know you can tell… I know you can see what's going to happen. You did it before."

Nothing.

"Tell me about my son."

The crisp smell of snow on the air.

"Can you? Are you there? Please, please, please come back and talk to me. Hello? Are you there?"

Jim slumped forward, head in his hands. He'd put up a brave front for so long, fought Joyce and her fatalistic acceptance. He'd torn his life apart, excised that hopelessness. But it had spread so far. And now, here in the cold and the dark, it found him again.

For a very long time, there was nothing but the sound of his sobs in the playground.

When he finished crying, Jim raised his head and said "Hi."

The boy in the red sweater was there. "Hello."

"I thought…" Jim's voice cracked. "I thought you left."

"Not yet."

Jim nodded. "When we got here, I thought 'Oh god, what if he's finished and there's no…'"

"…I'm not finished." The boy stuck his hands in his pockets.

Jim stood up. "Can I help you dig?"

The boy shook his head. "Ground's too hard."

Frozen, waiting for spring. Jim nodded.

In the cold, semi-dark, the playground looked like something from an old movie. Monochrome. Everything cut from black and gray construction paper.

Except for the boy's bright face, very pale.

"Aren't you cold?"

"No," the boy replied. "I don't get cold anymore."

Jim wondered what the boy could feel, wondered how long it had been since he'd felt anything—the chill of winter, the warmth of the sun on his back? How many years, how many seasons had come and gone?

How many more would there be, before he was done?

Jim decided there were some things he didn't really want to know, when it came right down to it. There were some questions you just shouldn't ask.

And that wasn't why he'd come. "Can you help me?"

The boy didn't answer, looked away.

Jim got out his cigarettes.

The boy's face twisted. "I don't like those."

Jim considered the cigarette between his fingers. "Yeah. I don't much either."

"Then why do you do it?"

"I don't know. It'll kill you, I know." Jim shrugged. "I don't know." He dropped the cigarette, ground it into the frozen earth with the toe of his shoe.

"My son is dying." It was a fact. No amount of arguing with his ex-wife, no carefully worded answers to the questions James kept asking him… none of it would change the truth of that. No matter what he tried, no matter how much he hoped, no matter if the impossible happened and the treatment worked and everything turned out all right in the end… the truth was that, as of this moment, his son was dying.

"I have to watch him…" Jim waited until the moment passed. "He has to take that fucking poison again in a few days."

"Poison?"

Jim didn't know how to explain modern medicine to a child from god-only-knows when. "It's like medicine, very strong medicine to kill the bad things inside him."

He took a breath. "Everyone lies to him, including me. I lie to him. I tell him that it'll make him better. I tell him he has to do it, that he'll feel better after… but it's not true. He's sicker than ever and all his hair's fallen out and he can't eat or sleep and…"

He crushed the dead cigarette again, grinding at it with his heel. Just because.

He looked at the boy standing there in front of him, a boy that he had no explanation for, no word to describe except a very silly one—"ghost"—and that wasn't nearly enough to hang all his hopes on.

But it was all he had.

"Is he going to die?" He was pleading, he knew. He could hear it in his voice. So be it. He would beg if he had to. "Please. I don't want him to die."

The boy said nothing, his mouth worked briefly for a moment. His lips tightened, very white.

"Something bad happened to you, didn't it?" Jim asked. "You died."

The boy nodded.

"How..?" Jim stopped himself, not certain he wanted to know.

He needed to know. "How long ago?"

"I don't know."

"How old are..?" Jim checked himself. "How old were you when you..?"

But the boy turned away.

"Wait." Jim held up his hand. He didn't know what he would do if the boy just simply walked back into the night. "I'm sorry. Please?"

The boy shook his head. "I can't remember."

"But you do remember some things? Can you remember your mother? Did you have brothers and sisters? Did you have friends? Did you go to school?" Jim could feel the panic, his words getting away from him. He knew he was running the risk of pushing the boy away, driving him back to wherever he came from.

He didn't care. He had to try. For James.

"I need to know." Jim raised his palms. "My son is sick. He's dying. And I want to know if…"

No hesitation in the boy's voice. "Everyone dies."

Jim nodded. "What's it like?"

"It's bad."

Jim shook his head. "After. What's it like after?"

The boy looked at him. "I don't know."

Jim tried very hard not to let his words get away from him again, failed. "Is he going to die? Is he? Will you tell me? I know you know, I know you can tell. Tell me."

He sat down again, too frantic to keep standing. He put his fingers through the slats of the bench, holding tight, grounding himself, pushing roots into the frozen earth. "I don't want him to… will I have to… oh God, I don't want to have to watch him die."

"You won't."

Jim looked at the boy, afraid of that little flicker. Afraid to hope. "What do you mean? Is he going to die, but I won't see it. Will I be there?"

"No." The boy shook his head. "You won't."

Jim let out a long, shuddering sigh. "God, if he's going to die I want to be there. But I don't want him to die."

"Jimmy," the boy, gentler this time. "Everyone dies."

"But not now." Jim wanted to grab the boy, to shake him and force him to change it somehow. "I don't care if he dies when he's old, after I'm gone, after he's lived his whole life. Fine with me, but not until…"

"…he dies after you're gone."

Jim had his answer.

"What's it like?"

The boy would not meet his eyes.

"Tell me," Jim said. "After. What's it like?"

"I don't know." The boy shook his head. "It's… lonely. Not at first. My friends would still come and play here sometimes, but they couldn't see me. Once…" The boy's eyes filled.

He's crying, Jim realized. *Oh dear God, ghosts can cry.*

The boy drifted here and there around the playground, his words soft and sad as snow. "Once… my mother came. With my father. They had… they had a baby with them. A little sister. They just sat for a while and watched everybody playing. Then my mother started crying and my father, he… he took her home. They didn't come back."

The boy stopped, dug at the frozen ground with the toe of his shoe.

Jim understood. The boy couldn't dig, couldn't do anything but wander. Restless until the thaw came.

"My friends got older. They were taller… Then they were gone. For a while there were other children I could play with. Some of them couldn't see me. Some helped me dig, like you did."

He drifted close, reached out as though he might touch Jimmy's hand… and then moved away once more.

"But they don't come here, not any more. Sometimes people come here to drink and… other things. But I don't, I don't let them see me.

They're..."

The boy stopped and looked at Jim. He smiled, put out his hand and touched Jim's cheek.

Jim started at the flash of cold, of wetness on his skin.

"You have snow on your face."

Jim looked up. The air was full of fat slow flakes drifting down. He hadn't noticed, hadn't noticed the soft gentle sound as it fell all around him.

It was warmer now, somehow.

"You know," he leaned back on the bench. "You can only get so cold. After a while, you start to get warm again."

The boy studied him, curiosity flickering across his face. "Are you cold?"

Jim considered. "Not cold enough to be warm. Not yet."

"You should go home."

Jim shook his head, his face turned upward, snow gathering on his eyelashes. Cold tears. "It's not home. It's just an empty place."

He slipped off his glove and opened his hand, watching the snow gather and melt. "I left my home."

"Why?"

"I don't know." Jim could feel it now, the cold radiating up his fingertips, lacing across his palm and into his wrist. "It was an awful thing to do, I know. But I couldn't, I just couldn't stay."

He didn't know how to explain the way it felt, to work so hard to keep James hopeful, while his mother eroded everything, crumbling the edges of the foundation he tried so hard to lay for their son.

"I could stay here." He looked around. "This is a good place."

"You'd freeze."

"Just like Walt Disney." Jim smiled softly.

"Mickey Mouse..." The boy, very far away.

Jim's hand was almost full now. Only the tips of his fingers showed, outraged and pink at the cold.

"Is James going to die?" Jim did not look up at the boy, did not want to give him a chance to tell another half-truth.

The boy in the red sweater said nothing.

Jim nodded. "Will I see him again? Afterward? Does that even happen?"

The boy looked away.

Jim tried very hard not to cry. "I'd be okay if I knew for sure that I'd be waiting for him. I'd be okay knowing that I'd be there when he..."

He stopped and raised his hand toward the boy, as though to touch him. "But you said I die before him, didn't you?"

The boy would not look at him.

Jim lowered his hand, crushed the snow in his fist. The cold, lacing into his bones. "I know you didn't say it. But that's what you told me. Isn't it?"

Finally, the boy turned back—his face, very pale in the dark.

He nodded.

Jim sat back, thoughts drifting. Snowflakes.

"That would be all right with me. If I knew that he would have someone waiting for him, if I could get there first and be waiting for him when..."

"...you're cold." The boy reached forward and wiped snow off of Jim's face.

"I could stand it," Jim went on. "Knowing that he'd have me there."

"Jimmy..."

"...listen," Jim smiled. "You can hear the snow."

The boy nodded. "Yes."

Jim closed his eyes. "That's my favorite sound in the whole world. You hear how quiet it is? I love that sound. How does it do that? Why does it get quieter when it snows?"

"I don't know."

Jim felt a thick flake of snow land at the corner of his mouth. He didn't bother brushing it away. He could feel more, melting into his scalp.

"God, I'd give anything to stay here for the rest of my life and listen to the snow."

He opened his eyes.

The boy was still there.

Jim smiled.

"It's so quiet," he said. "Can you hear it?"

The boy nodded.

"Oh, listen…"

Jim closed his eyes again.

The boy in the red sweater sat down on the bench next to Jim. He leaned over, laying his head on the man's shoulder.

Jim began to cry. "Oh god, god, god, god… I don't want him to be alone."

The boy reached up again to wipe the snow from Jim's face.

He settled back, his head against Jim's shoulder once more and watched the snow fall while the man cried.

DAWN

It snowed through the night, transforming the playground by morning. Everything rounded over. Smooth, featureless.

You could get lost there. Unless you knew where things were, knew what slept beneath the mounds. Only the slide and the tops of the swings were visible, the chains rising up out of the deep drifts below.

The boy in the red sweater sat on the bench, a mound of snow next to him.

White drifts all around, like clouds.

Trees heavy with winter.

Dark sky above, more snow on the way.

He longed to dig, to feel the warm sun on his back and hear the calls of the children around him.

The boy held his hands in his lap and he wept.

It was so long until spring.

AKNOWLEDGEMENTS

This project was a long time coming. It took nearly twenty years to go from its earliest incarnation as a stage play to the book you now hold in your hands. Along the way, I had a lot of help. And I'm grateful for all of it.

Many thanks to Dark Gracie, Dona Hall, Wes Covey, Craig Huston, Priscilla Giuseffi, and Mary Ricci for graciously volunteering as test readers early on.

And I owe a great deal to Kyle Harris for being so generous with his creativity and time as he put together the design and layout for this book. Kyle once said to me that "Design solves a problem" and he certainly solved a number of mine on this project.

Most of all, I want to thank Keeley Geary for all of her love and encouragement over the years. I am grateful beyond all measure. May we start and end every day in each other's arms, my love, through all the seasons to come.

T.M. Camp
April 6, 2016
Grand Rapids, Michigan

ABOUT THE AUTHOR

As a child, T.M. Camp spent most of his time in a dreamworld. These days, he spends most of his time trying to get other people to join him there.

After thirty years of writing, he has over thirty plays, countless short stories and poems, and four novels to his name.

T.M. long ago gave up trying to write a fresh and clever biography with each new publication. In fact he didn't even bother to proofread this page after he gave it to me to lay out. What an idiot.

T.M. lives in Michigan with his excellent, lovely wife and an indeterminate number of cats and children of variable age and intelligence.

The house they live in is very old and quite haunted.

www.ingramcontent.com/pod-product-compliance
Lightning Source LLC
Chambersburg PA
CBHW021126130626
46554CB00002B/880